BLOCKADE
RUNNER

Bonnets and Bugles Series · 5

BLOCKADE RUNNER

GILBERT MORRIS

MOODY PRESS

CHICAGO

ISBN: 0-8024-0915-6

3 5 7 9 10 8 6 4 2

Printed in the United States of America

To Laura—
fairest of ten thousand!

Contents

1

A Grown-up Party

Oh, no, Leah, I think your dress is much prettier than mine!" Lucy Driscoll turned her head to one side, touched her dimple with a forefinger, and nodded with a smile. "That green matches your eyes exactly."

Leah Carter flushed with pleasure and examined herself in the mirror. She was wearing a muslin dress printed in a paisley pattern of coral and white with green trim on the collar and sleeves. Her skirt was in three tiers and very full.

She touched her honey-colored hair, which was done up in the newest fashion, and her eyes glowed with excitement. Nevertheless, she quickly said, "Well, I don't think it's as pretty as yours, Lucy."

She was accustomed to being second in any competition regarding clothing, for Lucy Driscoll was the daughter of John and Edith Driscoll, one of the wealthiest planter families in the Richmond area. Lucy *was* a beautiful girl—small, well-shaped, and her blonde hair and blue eyes exactly what they should be. The dress she wore was more ornate than most grown women wore and was made of green silk with pink lace flounces.

Leah had come to pay Lucy a weeklong visit. As the two girls giggled and dressed and arranged each other's hair, Leah thought how strange it was that they had become friends, for they had not always been on such good terms.

9

Lucy Driscoll was a Rebel to the core, believing in the Southern Confederacy with all her heart. Leah, on the other hand, came from Kentucky, a border state. Her brother was in the Union army, and her father was a sutler, serving the Union troops. The two girls had not been at all friendly at first, but Lucy had changed greatly, Leah thought, smiling.

"It's so nice that you invited me to stay with you, Lucy." Leah smiled. "Do you think we dare wear some of that rice powder you found?"

Lucy giggled. "I don't see why not. After all, we're practically grown up. I mean, after all, we're fourteen years old, going on fifteen."

The two girls delved into the cosmetics that had belonged to Lucy's sister, and finally Lucy exclaimed, "We'd better go down! I think I hear the music already."

"I wouldn't want to be late," Leah said.

Lucy's eyes gleamed. "I would!" she exclaimed. "If you go to a party early, nobody notices you— but when you go in late like this, everybody stops to stare." She laughed and took Leah by the arm. "I'm just joking, but I'm so excited—our first grown-up ball! And some of the young officers will ask us to dance."

"I'm more excited about meeting Belle Boyd than any officers," Leah said. "I mean, she's the most famous Confederate spy in the whole South. She's a real celebrity."

"Oh, it'll be fun meeting her all right."

Lucy was rather spoiled with meeting celebrities. She had met Jefferson Davis, Robert E. Lee, Stonewall Jackson, and Jeb Stuart. They had all been at her parents' home at one time or another.

"I'm more excited about this dance card," she said. Lucy held up her card, and her eyes sparkled. "How many dances are you going to give Cecil?"

Leah flushed slightly. "Oh, I don't know," she muttered. She was much shyer than Lucy, having grown up on a farm. She'd had no experience in ballroom dancing at all until she came to take care of her Uncle Silas here in Virginia. Trying now to look casual about the whole thing, she said, "He probably won't even ask me—not with you around in that dress."

"Oh, yes, he will. He's crazy about you, Leah." Lucy nodded. She was a Southern belle to the bone, having grown up with beaus and parties and balls. Her older sister had been the most beautiful eligible belle in Richmond, so Lucy was fully aware of all the ways of flirting with young men.

They went down the beautiful curving staircase where they encountered a couple who had just entered.

"I don't believe you've met Mr. and Mrs. Pollard, have you, Leah?" Lucy said. "Mr. Pollard is the editor of the *Richmond Examiner*." She reached over and patted the big man's hand. "He's not only the best-looking editor in the South but the most important."

John Pollard was a tall, portly man with longish gray hair and brown, friendly eyes. "Now, don't you start flirting with me," he teased Lucy. "My wife will be jealous."

Mrs. Pollard was a small woman with carefully dressed reddish hair and very light blue eyes. She smiled. "If he were a few years younger, I'd take him away right now." She turned to Leah and said,

"I've heard so much about you from your Uncle Silas. How is your family in Kentucky?"

"Oh, they're fine. I miss them a great deal, of course."

"I'm sure you do. Well—"

Mrs. Pollard was interrupted when a tall young man with the blackest possible hair, black as a crow's wing, joined them. He had well-set black eyes and was tanned in a very attractive fashion so that his teeth shone when he smiled.

"Why, hello, Jeff!" Lucy said quickly. "Have you met Mr. and Mrs. Pollard?"

The introductions were made, and Mr. Pollard examined Jeff's uniform. It was ash gray with brass buttons and looked very good on him. "What's your unit, soldier?"

"I'm in the Stonewall Brigade," Jeff Majors said proudly.

"You look so young!" Mrs. Pollard said.

"I'm almost sixteen," Jeff said quickly. "I'm a drummer boy right now, but it won't be long before I'll be in the regular army."

He turned to the two girls. "I've come to get my name on your programs before those other fellows get all the dances." He grinned. "Put me down for half of them."

Lucy laughed. "Why, you bold thing! I won't do any such thing as that—but you can have two."

Jeff winked at her, then turned to Leah. The two had grown up together, and their families were closely intertwined. As a matter of fact, Leah's family was keeping Jeff's baby sister, Esther. Since Jeff's mother had died and there had been no one else to care for the baby, the Carter family had generously volunteered.

"Well, I'll have all of yours then, Leah."

"No, you won't."

Another young man, dressed in a beautifully tailored brown suit, shoved his way in front of Jeff. "I'm having the dances with Leah. You may be in the army, but you can't hog all the good-looking girls."

Cecil Taylor was the same age as Jeff. He was rather thin with chestnut hair and bright blue eyes. His parents were almost as wealthy as Lucy's, and of course the two sets of parents had often whispered about how nice it would be if Cecil and Lucy fell in love and got married. Then, together they would have the biggest plantation in the South.

Mr. and Mrs. Pollard drifted away, and the two boys began to argue over dances. But they were soon swamped by soldiers. The two girls were young, but girls in the South matured early, and the young lieutenants themselves were mostly not over seventeen or eighteen.

Lucy had her arm seized by Jeff, who led her off to the dance floor. She looked back over her shoulder and smiled at Cecil, whereupon Jeff said sharply, "You watch out for that Cecil. He's not always a gentleman such as a young man should be."

"Don't you worry," Cecil retorted. "Jeff's the one to look out for." Turning to Leah, he said, "There's the music. I've got me the prettiest girl in Richmond, and I propose to have her all to myself as much as possible."

It was a beautiful experience for Leah. As she whirled around the floor, her hoop skirt swinging, she remembered that the first time she had come to this place it had not been so. She had come wearing rather plain clothes, and Lucy had cruelly interrogated her about her Northern sympathies.

Now, however, she was having a wonderful time. The oak floor was polished, and lights glistened from the chandeliers. At the sides of the room, silver trays and crystal glasses were lined up on a snow-white tablecloth along with all sorts of refreshment.

"You'd never know a war was going on, would you?" Cecil murmured.

Leah thought of the wounded soldiers she had visited in the hospital at Chimborazo. They had been so pathetic that sometimes she had to leave so that they could not see the tears that came to her eyes.

Looking around the ballroom, she thought about how, even on the streets of Richmond, clothes were wearing thin, groceries were nonexistent in some cases, and the Confederacy was slowly being squeezed to death by the blockade that the Union had thrown along the coastline. Only a few swift-sailing blockade runners dared brave the Yankee gunboats to carry cotton for sale in England, returning with the precious commodities that kept the South alive.

"No, you wouldn't know there's a war. This is very nice." She looked over to where Jeff was dancing with Lucy. He was very tall, and Lucy was so small that she had to look up at him. "I wish I were tiny like Lucy," Leah said suddenly. "I feel like a big old cow!"

Cecil stared at her in surprise, "What makes you think such a thing?"

"Oh, I don't know. I just feel that way."

"Well," Cecil said, "stop thinking that way." He glanced over and said, "They do make a nice-looking couple, don't they? Wouldn't be surprised but what Jeff didn't fall in love with her. Most fellows do. I did!"

"Oh, you two were just childhood playmates."

"Well, that's true enough, and I guess people don't often fall in love with people they grew up next door to."

"Sometimes they do."

Leah's answer was so short that Cecil stared at her. Then he seemed to suddenly remember that Leah and Jeff had grown up together just as he and Lucy had. "You know, I think you're stuck on Jeff."

Leah blushed and bit her lip. "Don't be silly," she said.

Just at that moment the band reached the end of the piece, and Leah was claimed by a short, fat young lieutenant with a moon face and a thick Southern accent. He could not dance very well, but he was amusing. Leah found herself laughing at some of his outlandish remarks.

The dance had been going on for thirty minutes when a woman came into the room in the company of Mr. and Mrs. Pollard. Lucy and Leah were at the table with Cecil and Jeff, sampling the punch.

"Look! There's Belle Boyd," Lucy said. "Come on, let's go meet her." They crossed the room, and when they reached the threesome, Lucy smiled and said, "Miss Boyd, I've just *got* to meet you. My name is Lucy Driscoll." She introduced her friends quickly and added, "Oh, Miss Belle, we've heard so much about you!"

Belle Boyd, a young woman of about twenty, was not really beautiful. Her nose was a little too prominent, and she had a very determined chin. But she had a trim figure, and her dark hair was worn in curls. Her best feature was her fine, dark blue eyes, which she now put on the young people in front of her. "I'm happy to meet all of you," she said.

"Oh, tell us about some of your adventures saving the Stonewall Brigade," Lucy said quickly. She turned to Jeff. "Jeff is in the Stonewall Brigade, and so are his father and his brother."

"Now here!" Mr. Pollard exclaimed. "We don't have time for Miss Boyd to tell stories."

He was right, for the young officers in their ash gray uniforms began crowding around, all clamoring for a dance with Miss Belle Boyd. She was sometimes called the Siren of the Shenandoah, sometimes the Rebel Spy. Already she had been arrested four times by Union authorities but each time had managed to obtain her freedom. She again turned her wonderful eyes on Leah, Lucy, and Jeff, saying quickly, "I'll be staying for a visit with your parents, Lucy. We'll have plenty of time to talk."

As Belle Boyd whirled off in the arms of a tall captain, Lucy said, "Isn't that exciting! She's so pretty!"

"She's not as pretty as you," Jeff observed. "Come on, this is my dance, Lucy." They moved away, Lucy's dress sweeping in wide circles to the waltz tune that the band played.

"Well, that's exciting—to get to meet Belle Boyd and actually talk to her. She's really something!" Jeff said.

"Yes, she is. I read stories about her in some of the magazines, but I never thought I'd get to meet her."

Leah's head was swimming from all the dances she'd had. She could not remember the names of all the young men she'd met.

Finally Cecil whispered, "Let's go get some more refreshments."

He got some cake and punch, handed a plate and cup to Leah, and said, "Come on, let's get out of this noise. I haven't had a chance to talk to you for all these blasted soldiers!"

"Don't call them that!" Leah protested.

She followed him out into a small garden area paved with flagstone. When he closed the French doors, the music became soft and muted. "Hey, this is nice, isn't it? Here, let's sit on this bench!"

Leah sat down and took a bite of cake. "This is good," she said. She looked around and noted the huge trees surrounding the Driscoll mansion. "I love magnolias," she said. "Their blossoms smell sweeter than anything."

Cecil took a swallow of punch and turned to her. "No better than you. They don't smell any better than you. You've been using perfume."

Leah flushed, for she had used some of the scent that Lucy had appropriated from her sister. "That's not nice to talk about what a girl smells like."

Cecil grinned. He was a happy-go-lucky boy. "Well, it is if they smell good," he argued.

Leah liked Cecil a great deal. He was an alert young man, full of fun and oftentimes practical jokes, and she enjoyed his teasing. He began talking about how in another two years he would be able to join the army.

Leah said quickly, "Oh, I hope the war's over by that time."

"Well, if the Yankees give up, it will be," Cecil said confidently.

"I don't know—the South is losing so many men."

"So are the blue bellies."

"I know, but they have so many more. Their armies just keep filling up."

"Sometimes numbers don't count so much."

"What does that mean?"

"Well, in the story about Gideon in the Bible, the Israelites only had about three hundred men—and they defeated their enemies."

"That's not the same thing!"

"Why not?"

"Because that happened a long time ago!"

"Well then, look at the American Revolution. The British had more soldiers than the colonists—but they didn't win." Cecil suddenly asked, "Which side are you really for, Leah? I've never really understood that. I mean, your brother's in the Union army, and Jeff's in the Confederate army. You've got an uncle here that's for the South. But your family—I guess they have to be for the North. What about you?"

It was a question that Leah had never been able to answer. She hated the idea of slavery with all of her heart. She also hated the war. But it had been obvious for some time that the North and the South would never be reconciled by peaceful means.

"I don't know," she finally said and dropped her head. "I just wish it were over."

Cecil was a sensitive young man. He obviously saw that he had disturbed her with his talk of the war and was sorry for it. Then his eyes gleamed with humor, and he said, "Leah!" He put down his cup. "I made my mother a promise one time. Do you think you ought to keep your promises? Especially to your mother?"

"Why, of course I do." Leah grew curious. "What did you promise her?"

"I promised her I would never kiss a girl until I was seventeen."

"Well, I think that's good." Leah nodded firmly.

Cecil reached over and took her arms. He was laughing as he said, "But I've decided to make an exception in your case." Then, before she could move, he kissed her on the lips.

Just as he did, the door opened behind them.

Leah pulled away from Cecil and leaped to her feet.

There stood Jeff with Lucy, staring at them. Lucy hid a smile behind her hand, but Jeff's dark eyes were angry. He said, "I think it's about time for you two to come inside."

"Oh, don't be such an old stick, Jeff." Lucy said.

But Jeff turned and walked away, and she followed him.

"I sure made old Jeff mad that time, didn't I?" Cecil whistled softly. He stared at Leah, saying, "I'm sorry. I was just teasing."

"Oh, he'll be all right. Jeff's just got kind of a hot temper."

Later on, Leah found it was not all right. She had one more dance with Jeff, and he did not say a word to her. He kept his head high and his eyes fixed over her head at the other dancers.

"Don't be mad, Jeff. Cecil was just teasing."

"None of my business what you do!" he said shortly. "If you want to go around kissing everybody that comes along—well, that's fine with me! 'Course, I expect your family would be pretty disappointed in you if they found out."

Instantly Leah grew angry. "I suppose you're going to run and write a letter telling them—or perhaps tell Uncle Silas!"

"Well, somebody needs to tell them."

"You're just an old tattletale! Besides, I bet you kissed Lucy, didn't you?"

Jeff's face suddenly flushed. "That's none of your business," he said. "I'm older than you are."

"One year older! That makes you grown up, does it?"

"It means I'm older than you are!"

"That doesn't mean anything!"

Jeff grew more angry. "You have a stubborn streak in you. Everybody knows that."

"*I* have a stubborn streak?" Leah glared at him, her eyes flashing. "You're the one who's stubborn—and unreasonable too!"

"You think it's reasonable to kiss a boy out in the garden?"

Actually Leah was not proud of her scene with Cecil, but as many people do when they're feeling guilty, she tried to cover up her feelings by attacking others. "You're a fine one to talk! You made a fool of yourself over Lucy the first time you ever saw her."

"I never kissed her in the garden!"

"You would if you got the chance!"

20

"I would not!"

The argument flared up further, and finally Jeff turned and walked off.

That night, in the room the two girls shared, Lucy said cautiously, "Don't worry about Jeff. He'll be all right."

"I don't care if he is or not!" Leah said. She turned over and said no more. She was so angry and upset that tears came to her eyes, but she kept very still, not allowing Lucy to dream that she was crying.

For a long time she lay there, going over the terrible argument with Jeff, and finally admitted to herself that she'd been in the wrong—at least partially.

But we'll make it—we always do.

Yet somehow she felt worse than she had over the arguments she'd had with Jeff in the past. Finally she drifted off to sleep—and had bad dreams all night.

2

Belle Gives Some Advice

The day after the party, Leah remained alone and was very quiet for most of the day.

Lucy knew, of course, that she was disturbed about the scene with Jeff and tried to encourage her. She must have quickly realized, however, that Leah did not want to talk about the matter.

"I'm going for a ride," Lucy said. "Do you want to go with me?"

"No, I think I'll just stay and read."

"It might do you good, Leah."

"I don't think so. Maybe later."

After Lucy left, Leah went to the extensive family library, a huge room filled with books and magazines and papers of all kinds. She found a novel by James Fenimore Cooper and sat down in a horsehide chair beside a window. Soon she was immersed in the story and had managed to forget the dreadful scene with Jeff.

The door suddenly opened, and Belle Boyd walked in. "Oh!" she said. "I didn't know anyone was in here."

"It's just me—Leah." Getting up, she said, "I expect you'll be wanting to look for something to read."

Belle Boyd said, "Oh, I can do that anytime. Sit down and tell me about yourself."

"About myself? Why, there's nothing much to tell."

"I'll bet there is." Belle settled herself gracefully on the couch and smiled encouragingly. "Now, tell me about your home."

Leah sat down again and quickly sketched her background.

Belle seemed to find her story a little sad. She frowned and shook her head. "There are so many families divided by the war—but as soon as we win, that'll be over, and things'll be like they were."

Leah doubted it would be quite that simple, but she said, "Please, Miss Belle, tell me about some of your adventures. You've had so many of them!"

Belle Boyd acted as though she was accustomed to this. She laughed and said, "Are you planning on becoming a spy for the Confederacy, Leah?" It was clear that she loved to talk about her exploits and at once told about an exciting adventure.

"I'm not sure you'd like to hear *all* my adventures, Leah. I suppose you've heard about the time I had to shoot a Yankee soldier?" Her eyes gleamed.

"Why . . . no . . . I haven't."

"Well, a Federal search party began pillaging our home. We all took it as well as possible, but one of the soldiers began addressing me in a most offensive manner. He became so abusive I could stand it no longer!" Belle's eyes flashed with anger at the memory. "Finally my blood was boiling. I just drew my pistol and shot him!"

"Did he die?"

"Yes, he did. But he brought it on himself."

Leah was rather taken aback but asked for another story.

"Once Stonewall and his brigade were outside of Front Royal, but they had no idea of the strength of the Yankee force. I mounted my horse and rode until I encountered Major Henry Douglas, who was on a scouting mission. I was almost falling off my horse with weariness and had to press my hand against my heart, but I managed to say, 'Go back and tell General Jackson that the Yankee force is very small—one regiment of Maryland infantry, several pieces of artillery, and several companies of cavalry. Tell him I know, for I went through the Union camp and got it out of an officer. Tell him to charge right down, and he will catch them all. I must hurry back. Good-bye—my love to all the dear boys!' I remember I kissed my hand to Major Douglas as I rode away."

"And what happened, Miss Belle?"

"Why, General Jackson took Front Royal that afternoon. They routed the Yankees and took $300,000 in commissary stores!"

"And what happened then?"

"I was arrested as a spy and sent to the Old Capitol Prison in Washington."

Leah had sat enthralled while listening to Belle, who told her adventures well. She sighed and said, "You have a great deal of courage, Miss Belle. Not many women would have been able to do what you've done."

Belle glanced at her. She rather quietly changed the subject. "You look a little depressed, Leah. Is anything wrong?"

"Oh, no, it's nothing."

"Come on, now! Tell me about it. A pretty young girl like you—I expect I know what the problem is."

"Oh, it's nothing, really."

"I bet you've had a disagreement with some young man. Is that the way of it?"

Trapped, Leah dropped her eyes and began to pick at the pattern on her dress. She was wearing a simple tan cotton dress with a locket around her neck. "Oh, you wouldn't be interested."

When Belle saw Leah fingering the locket, she asked innocently, "Is there a picture inside that pretty locket?"

Leah felt herself flush, and Belle Boyd smiled even more broadly.

"Let me see it, will you?"

Leah reluctantly opened the locket and held it out. It contained the picture of Jeff Majors he had given her for a birthday present. That gold locket was her prized possession, but she felt uncomfortable showing the picture to Belle Boyd.

"Why, this is the young man that was at the party last night. What's his name?"

"Jeff Majors."

"Did you two quarrel?"

"Well . . . yes, we did," Leah admitted reluctantly.

"Tell me about it."

Suddenly Leah began to pour out her story. She had not been able to talk to Lucy because she secretly felt that Lucy admired Jeff.

But Belle Boyd seemed truly sympathetic. Her large eyes fixed firmly on Leah's face, and the girl told the whole story.

To Leah's horror she found that her own eyes were beginning to fill up with tears as she ended. "I—I don't know what's the matter with me. I'm getting to be a regular crybaby." She searched in her pocket, came up with a handkerchief, and dabbed at her eyes. "I never used to cry when I was little. Now look at me—blubbering like anything!"

Belle leaned over and patted Leah's arm. "How old are you, Leah?"

"Fourteen. Going on fifteen," she amended quickly.

"Well, it's not too strange that you would be easily disturbed."

"But I never got disturbed when I was little. My parents always would say, 'Everybody else may get excited but not Leah—she's steady as a rock.'"

"You were a little girl then, but something's happening to you now, and you have to understand it."

"What is it? What do you mean?" Leah asked, mystified.

"Well, you're moving out of girlhood," Belle said quietly, "and sometimes it's hard to stop being a little girl. Being little is safe."

Leah was fascinated. "What do you mean by that, Miss Belle?"

"I mean, when you're a little girl and you have problems, you can take them to your parents to resolve. And your problems are usually pretty simple: will I get a new dress, will I get a new doll, can I go on the picnic? Things like that. But at your age, that's changing."

Leah knew Miss Boyd was young enough to remember clearly when she was Leah's age, and now she told about how it had been. "When I was just your age, it was very hard for me. For one thing, I was changing physically—and that was *very* confusing."

Leah understood.

"But what happens inside is even harder to understand." She sighed and shrugged her trim shoulders. "It's hard to stop being a little girl, Leah, but you have to become a woman. There's no way around that."

Leah twisted her handkerchief nervously. She knew what Belle Boyd was trying to tell her. She had already thought of such things, and her mother had talked with her. But somehow Belle was able to make it all come clear.

The two talked for a long time. When they finally stood up, Belle put her arms around the girl, hugged her, and kissed her cheek. "You're so pretty, Leah. You're a beautiful young woman. It may be hard right now, but things will come out all right. Jeff's just a little jealous." She laughed and said, "I can tell you a few things about how to make men jealous—and how to get them over it."

"I don't think I want to know that—at least not how to make them jealous," Leah said quickly, "but I would like to know how not to get into these things."

"You probably will get into some more as you grow up. That's part of being a woman."

As Belle turned to go, Leah asked, "How long will you be here, Miss Belle?"

At once Belle Boyd looked a little uncomfortable. "Well, I'm not sure," she said evasively. "I do have some things to do. But my plans aren't complete yet."

Belle left the room, and Leah thought, *I wonder why she was so secretive?* And then she thought instantly, *I bet she's going on some kind of secret mission!*

For the next two days, Leah stayed close to Belle. Several times she thought that she sensed an air of mystery around the Rebel Spy. Belle would start to say something, then break off abruptly and change the subject.

At dusk one afternoon, Leah went out into the rose garden. She seated herself on a low bench and was watching the sun go down. The garden was thickly planted with rosebushes that had grown very high, and there were paths between them. And then she heard Mr. Pollard's voice.

"We must be very careful, my dear. You know the dangers."

"Of course, Mr. Pollard." It was Belle Boyd speaking, and instantly Leah knew that they were discussing some sort of assignment.

The voices came closer.

Then Mr. Pollard said, "Have you told anyone about the journey?"

"No one knows except President Davis."

"It's a very dangerous thing, but I think it will be a worthy mission for you."

"I'll give you the particulars of the—" Suddenly Belle broke off, for they had turned the corner and saw Leah sitting on the bench. "Leah!" she exclaimed, "I didn't know you were out here!"

"I just . . . came out to watch the sunset." Leah stood to her feet.

Mr. Pollard was disturbed. "Did you hear what we were talking about, Leah?"

She saw that Belle was watching her carefully, though she said nothing.

Leah was a very truthful girl. "Yes, I did, Mr. Pollard—about Miss Belle going on a journey."

Belle and Mr. Pollard exchanged glances.

Mr. Pollard said severely, "I wish you hadn't heard us, Leah."

"I wasn't eavesdropping—really I wasn't."

Belle came over to her. She examined Leah's face. She was unsmiling this time. "It will be very dangerous for me if anyone knew I was going on this trip. If I were caught, I'd be sent back to prison —perhaps for life."

"Oh, I wouldn't like that at all—it would be terrible for you," Leah said.

"I've got to get to England—on a very important mission."

"Yes," Mr. Pollard nodded. "It would be very bad for the Confederacy if she were captured."

"You're going to England?"

"Oh, you didn't overhear all of the plan? Well, you might as well know," Belle said. "I'm going to England to try to raise support for the Confederacy. If the Yankees knew I was on that blockade runner, they'd throw every ship they had into the area to try to capture it."

Leah said quickly, "I won't say a word—not to anyone in the whole world. I promise, Miss Belle."

Belle looked at the girl and seemed to find what she was looking for. "I'm sure you won't," she said. She turned to Mr. Pollard, saying confidently, "It'll be all right. Leah and I are good friends. She won't say anything. We can trust Leah."

Mr. Pollard seemed relieved. "That's good. It will only be for a day or two, Leah." He patted her on the shoulder and said, "I'm sorry you had to get involved in this, but just don't say anything to anyone and it'll be all right."

After the two left, Leah walked slowly along the pathways. The scent of the roses filled the air, and the night air was still. Far off she heard someone singing a song in a plaintive voice. She thought, *I'm glad I don't have to be a spy like Belle Boyd. It'd be exciting, but I wouldn't like it!*

3

"You're Acting Like a Spoiled Brat!"

J eff, I don't know what's the matter with you!"

Captain Nelson Majors stared across the tent at his son. His skin was darkly tanned, and he had hazel eyes that seemed to penetrate whatever he looked at. He had a black mustache, and his eyebrows matched. He had been called one of the "Black Majorses" back in Kentucky where he grew up.

He stood tall now in his captain's uniform with the Engineers insignia on his shoulder.

"You've been going around like a whipped puppy for a week. I know the army's not doing very much right now, but these are the times we get ready for the battle that's to come. Now what's the matter with you, Jeff?"

"Well . . ." Jeff hated to admit that he had had another disagreement with Leah—the two had had arguments before, because both of them were very sensitive—but finally he could not bear the weight of his father's glance. "Oh, Leah and I had a fight," he finally admitted.

"Can't you two ever get along? What is it this time?"

Jeff flushed. He refused to tell what had actually happened. He finally mumbled, "Oh, you know how girls are. A fellow can't get along with them!"

"Well, I know how *you* are!" the captain said, glaring at his son. "You're acting like a spoiled brat! I'm downright ashamed of the way you behave sometimes!"

Jeff was ready to end the conversation long before his father was. He loved his father dearly, and, since the loss of his mother, they had been especially close.

The two of them, along with Tom, Jeff's nineteen-year-old brother, were in the Stonewall Brigade. This was not unusual, for brothers and fathers and sons often tried to stay in the same outfit. But now, with his father still berating him, Jeff wished he would finish.

In the middle of a sentence, a voice called out, "Captain Majors!"

The captain looked toward the tent flap, and a look of pleasure came over his face. "George Bier! What in the world are you doing in Richmond?"

The man who entered, Jeff had never seen before. He was short, had black hair, a short black beard, and a pair of direct gray eyes. He was wearing a naval uniform. He shook hands with Capt. Majors, then turned as the captain introduced his son.

"This is Jeff, my son," Majors said. "I don't think you've met him."

"Glad to know you, Jeff."

"Glad to know you, sir."

"You're in the Stonewall Brigade too?"

"Yes, sir. I'm a drummer boy."

"Fine—fine! I was on Jackson's staff myself, but now I'm just a humble sailor."

"Captain Bier's one of the blockade runners—the best of them, I think," Jeff's father explained.

"Don't get him talking about his ship, the *Grey-hound*. He'll bore you to death!"

Bier laughed roughly. "A captain that's not proud of his ship isn't worth much," he said. "Well, are you going to feed me or not?"

Entertaining Captain Bier turned out to be a pleasure for Jeff. He was one of Nelson Majors's old friends. The two had been together at West Point, but both had chosen to fight for the South. Bier, indeed, had been a soldier for a brief time but was far more useful to the Confederacy in running the blockade.

Jeff had little to do, and Bier stayed overnight. After Captain Majors had gone to bed, Bier said, "I can't sleep yet, Jeff. Show me around the camp."

The two of them strolled through the encampment, then came back to the tent that Bier had been assigned. "Sit down and talk with me awhile."

Jeff was glad enough to do so, for he was not sleepy either. "Where's your ship?" he asked.

"In Wilmington."

"Wilmington? That's up by the Cape Fear River, isn't it?"

"Well, you know your geography, I see. That's the best harbor we've got now."

"Wilmington is?"

"Why, yes. Look here, Jeff . . ." Captain Bier pulled out a sheet of paper and found a stub of pencil in his pocket. "Wilmington is seventeen miles up the Cape Fear River. See? And that river divides into two channels—both of them protected by the guns of Fort Fisher and Fort Caswell. That means that the Yankees have to use two blockading fleets to cover the coast—almost fifty ships. Well, we've

33

got a shallow coast—lots of little islands to dodge around—which makes it pretty nice for us who run the blockade."

Jeff said, "That makes sense, all right. I sure wish I could go on a ship sometime."

"Yes, it's a fine life. Of course, we get criticized for making money." A humorous light touched the captain's eyes, and he added, "I really don't think I'm all that greedy, but I admit there *is* a great deal of money to be made blockade running."

"I didn't know that, Captain. Just how much money is there in running the blockade?"

Captain Bier's eyes glowed. "Why, Jeff, one blockade runner turned a profit of $425,000 on a single round trip between Wilmington and Nassau!"

"Wow! He must be rich!"

"He retired on that one trip."

"That's pretty nice."

"Not bad for a simple captain."

"How much do sailors make on blockade runners?"

"Captains can get as much as $5,000 in gold for a round trip to Nassau. My chief engineer gets $2,500, and every member of the crew gets $250."

Jeff swallowed hard. "A private in the army gets only $14 a month."

"I know—and it's not right," Bier answered. "But then I stand the chance of losing my ship— my life savings."

"I can see that. And I know the Confederacy needs the powder and shot you bring back."

"Not all ships bring back war supplies, I'm afraid," the captain said. "The owner of the *Don* brought back one thousand pairs of corset stays."

"What!"

"I thought it was wrong, but Captain Hampden likes money. He also brought back a patent medicine from England that was supposed to cure liver ailments. It didn't, though. He sold the shipment in Nassau, or so I heard."

"Why would they want so many liver pills in Nassau?"

"Jeff, that place is a madhouse! Packed with sailors on leave, confidence men, cardsharpers—all with lots of money! They're a reckless lot, I tell you! Determined to eat, drink, and be merry with not a thought for anything else!"

The two talked far on into the night, and finally Captain Bier gave Jeff an odd look. "It's too bad you're in the army, in a way, Jeff."

"Why is that, sir?"

"Because I'm in need of another hand on the *Greyhound*. I could take you with me."

"But I'm not a sailor."

"The hand I need is more of a cabin boy. I need somebody to take care of my personal effects—take care of me, really."

"Why, I could do that!" Jeff exclaimed. The idea of going on a sea voyage suddenly struck him. "Say, I'd give anything if I could go with you—but it takes a long time to sail to England."

"Oh, I'm not going to England."

"You're not?"

"No, I'm going to Bermuda. Very few of the blockade runners go to England. I'll take a load of cotton to Bermuda and sell it to British brokers. Then I'll buy war supplies, medicine, and food and bring them right back to Wilmington." He gave Jeff another odd look, then said again, "Too bad you're in the army. It'd be an exciting trip for you—and it pays well."

Finally Jeff said good night, but he could not sleep. He tossed on his bunk until Charlie Bowers, his fellow drummer, mumbled, "I wish you'd be still, Jeff! Nobody can sleep with you thrashing around like that."

The next morning Jeff accosted his father at daybreak. "Captain, can I come in?" He remembered to use his father's military title.

"Well, come on."

Jeff walked into the tent to see his father shaving.

"What are you doing here this early, Jeff?"

"I talked to Captain Bier last night," he said carefully. He had thought this all out, and his eyes were gleaming. "He says he could use a cabin boy on his next voyage to Bermuda. I'd like to go with him."

"Why, you can't do that! You're in the army!"

"I know, but there's nothing to do right now," Jeff said plaintively. "You know we're not going anywhere for the next two weeks—not till the replacements get here and get trained. We'd be back long before then, Captain Bier said. We're just going to the Bahamas and right back."

Captain Majors brought the gleaming razor down over one cheek, wiped the lather on a cloth on his free arm, then turned to stare at Jeff. "I never heard of such a thing—a soldier going off on a vacation!"

"But it's for the Confederacy, Pa. You know how much good the blockade runners do."

"You're right there. If it weren't for them, we'd just about starve to death. We sure wouldn't have

36

any gunpowder." He continued to stare at his son. "You'd really like to go?"

"Pa, it would be so interesting—and he'd pay me too. I could send some money back to the Carters to take care of Esther."

Jeff knew this was a sore spot with his father. The captain's pay was very low, and it was in Confederate money. He was deeply grateful to the Carters for keeping Esther, but for a long time he had wanted to do something to defray their expenses.

"You'd like to do that, would you, Jeff?" he repeated.

"Yes, and we could send all the money back to Kentucky. It would pay for Esther's clothes and food and—why, everything, Pa." Excited, he again forgot to use his father's military title. "Can I go, Pa? Would it be all right?"

"Well, I'll think on it."

"Yes, sir."

Jeff knew better than to pressure his father, but somehow he thought it would happen.

Later that morning, his father stopped by where Jeff was cleaning his boots and said, "Jeff, I think it might be all right for you to make that trip. It would help financially, and it would be good for the cause too."

Jeff was overjoyed and went at once to Captain Bier's tent. "Captain, my father says I can go with you."

"Why, that's fine, Jeff. We'll make a sailor out of you—a short-term one. Wilmington, *Greyhound*, here we come!" He grinned at the boy, but then said, "People have been known to get hurt on these expeditions, but you're not afraid of that?"

"No, sir. It won't be as dangerous as being on a battlefield, and it'll be a lot more fun."

Captain Bier rubbed his chin. "Sometimes it's fun—and sometimes not so much fun. In any case, get your things together, and I'll show you what it's like to be a sailor."

4
Alarm at Midnight

Leah got out of the buggy and held the horses while Uncle Silas descended to the street. He held on very carefully, for he was still frail and not completely recovered from his long sickness. However, he was well enough to get out and had insisted on making a visit to the *Richmond Examiner*. He and Mr. John Pollard had been friends for years, and the two had not seen each other in some time.

As soon as Uncle Silas was safely out of the buggy, Leah wrapped the lines firmly, then leaped to the ground. She patted the mare's silky nose, saying, "There, Susie, I'll bring you something good before we go back home." Then she joined Uncle Silas and held his arm as they entered the *Examiner* office.

"I'll bet Mr. Pollard will be glad to see you, Uncle Silas."

"Yes, I've missed some of those checker games and arguments with him about his politics."

Uncle Silas was her father's uncle. He had grown so ill that Leah and her sister Sarah had come to Richmond to care for him.

Now as they entered the newspaper office, Mr. Pollard instantly came to greet them, wearing an apron that had once been white but was now almost completely covered with ink smears. He had a strange hat shading his eyes and several pens stuck in the pocket of the apron.

"Well, look who's here!" he said happily. "Silas Carter!" He shook Mr. Carter's hand enthusiastically. "Come right on back here and sit down. I was about ready to send out for some tea. We can take a break while I get your politics straightened out."

"You've been twenty-five years trying to do that." Uncle Silas smiled. He had white hair and beard and was still rather pale. He was, however, much healthier than he had been before Leah had come to nurse him.

"I'll go get the tea, Mr. Pollard," Leah said quickly. "You and Uncle Silas can talk."

She left the two men arguing loudly and happily over the Jefferson Davis administration. Going next door, she requested a pot of tea.

The proprietor, a tall slender woman with red hair, covered it with a cloth. "I fixed it just like Mr. Pollard likes it," she said, "and there's plenty for you and your uncle too. And I made those cakes just this morning."

Leah smiled. "They smell very good. I'll tell Uncle Silas you asked about him," she promised.

She returned to the office of the *Examiner*, and for the next hour she kept the two men liberally supplied with tea and cakes while they played checkers, loudly slamming the board victoriously or groaning in tragic voices.

"You two have more fun playing checkers than anybody I know." Leah always enjoyed it when her uncle had a good time. She knew he got lonely for his friends.

"That's because he's learned to beat me once in a while." Uncle Silas grinned. "When we first started playing I think we played five years before he won a game."

"That's not true!" Mr. Pollard exclaimed. "I think your memory's failing you, Silas!"

At that moment a clerk stuck his head in, his face smeared with ink. "We're out of paper again, Mr. Pollard. What're we going to do? Got to have paper!"

Pollard gritted his teeth. "Use those rolls of wallpaper," he said. "That's all we've got. And if that runs out, I guess we can use *old* wallpaper—tear it off the walls!"

When the clerk left, Silas stared at the editor. "Wallpaper?" he said. "You're printing a newspaper on *wallpaper?*"

"You wouldn't believe how hard it is to get paper, Silas. Just like everything else, it's in short supply. Getting harder and harder to make ends meet!"

His words seemed to cast a pall over the room, and Silas examined his friend's face curiously. "Looks like we're running out of about everything."

"Everything is about right! Can't buy the necessities of life anymore—and some of the junk those blockade runners bring back isn't worth bringing back."

"What kind of things would that be? I thought we needed everything," Leah asked.

"Captain Simms of the *Victory* brought back six cases of coffin nails. Coffin nails!" Mr. Pollard exclaimed. "Here we are needing quinine and medicine and food and gunpowder, and he brings back coffin nails!"

"Well," Uncle Silas said mildly, "I suppose there's a need for such things. After all, there's been enough coffins made around here." There was sadness in his voice. He shook it off. "How's your wife? I'm anxious to see her."

"Helen is not well." A frown came to Pollard's face. "It was a sudden thing. As a matter of fact, I don't know what I'm going to do. I have to leave her at home in order to publish this paper, and she's really not well enough to be left alone."

Silas said, "Why, you should have called on me, John."

"You? You're not a nurse."

"No, I'm not—but Leah here is." He smiled fondly at his great-niece. "I can testify to what a good nurse she is. Why, I had one foot in the grave practically when she and her sister Sarah came down from Kentucky." He related the story of how the two girls had routed the cantankerous woman housekeeper who was plaguing his life. "Ran her out of the house the day they got here." Silas grinned proudly. "I've been waited on hand and foot ever since."

"Well, I'd hate to see you lose your nurse, Silas." Mr. Pollard rubbed his chin thoughtfully and put his eyes on Leah. "But if you could spare this young lady for just a few days, it would take a load off my mind. As a matter of fact—" he broke off as if considering something deep in his mind "—I've got to make a business trip." He looked straight at Leah, and a thought passed between them.

He's going on that trip with Belle Boyd, Leah thought, *and he hates to leave his wife.*

At once she said, "Why, Mr. Pollard, I'd be happy to stay with Mrs. Pollard. Uncle Silas is able to take care of himself for the most part. Would it be for long?"

"Well, I'm hoping she'll be up and around in two or three days, but it might be as long as a week—or even two."

"Don't even think about it!" Silas put up his hand. "You still got that big old house out on the edge of town, haven't you?"

"Yes, I have."

"Well, if Mrs. Pollard could put up with me in the house, Leah and I could both stay there. That way—" he grinned "—she could take care of two patients instead of one."

"An excellent idea! That would certainly answer." Mr. Pollard was beaming then, and relief came into his face. "Would that be all right with you, Miss Leah?"

"Oh, yes. I'd be happy to do what I can, Mr. Pollard."

They spent some time talking about the arrangements. In the end, Leah and Uncle Silas picked up some clothes, Mr. Pollard got into his buggy, and they followed him to his house. It was a big frame dwelling with four bedrooms. The Pollards' two children were away at school, so there was no problem having a place to stay.

Mrs. Pollard, who was in bed, looked very feeble.

"Now, my dear, you're going to be all right," her husband said. "I brought you a fine nurse. You remember Miss Leah Carter from the ball at the Driscolls'."

Mrs. Pollard managed a faint smile. "Oh, I couldn't put you to all that trouble."

"Why, it's no trouble at all," Leah said quickly. "I'll be glad to stay with you, Mrs. Pollard."

"Yes, and she knows how to feed an invalid too." Silas smiled. "All kinds of soups and salads and—why, we'll have you out of that bed by the time your husband gets back, Helen!"

Mr. Pollard got them settled quickly, and Leah got acquainted with the kitchen.

At noon Mr. Pollard came to say good-bye. "You saved my life, Leah," he said gratefully. "I'll have to make this up to you somehow."

He said nothing of his trip, but Leah thought she knew what was on his mind. "You just go ahead and don't worry a bit about Mrs. Pollard," Leah said, smiling. "I'll see that she's well taken care of."

Leah was sleeping soundly when she heard the sound of a horse running at full speed. Sometimes there was traffic on the roads leading into Richmond as soldiers moved by. At times even caissons and guns rumbled past, but this time the galloping horse stopped just outside the house. Instantly she heard footsteps on the front porch and a hard banging on the front door.

"Who could that be?" she muttered. Throwing on a robe, she went to the door. "Who is it?"

"I've got a message for Mrs. Pollard."

Leah hesitated for a moment, then opened the door slightly. "Mr. Pollard's not here."

"I know that!" The man was wearing dusty clothes and had a hat pulled down over his eyes. Reaching into his pocket, he drew out an envelope and thrust it at Leah. "There! I had to ride hard to get here. Will you see that Mrs. Pollard gets it at once?"

"Yes, I'll do that."

"Thank you, Miss." The man turned abruptly, jumped off the porch, then leaped on his horse and rode off into the darkness.

Leah stood holding the envelope, wondering what to do. She closed and bolted the door, then walked down the hall thinking, *She really—if she's sleeping, I hate to disturb her.* But as she quietly opened Mrs. Pollard's door, Leah saw that she was awake.

Stepping inside the bedroom, she said, "Did the rider wake you?"

"Yes. What is it, Leah?"

"It's a message. The man didn't say his name." Moving over to the bed she handed the envelope to Mrs. Pollard, who struggled to sit up.

"Would you hand me my glasses, please, Leah?"

Mrs. Pollard placed the glasses on her nose and opened the envelope. She read the message silently, then Leah saw her hand begin to tremble.

"What is it, Mrs. Pollard? Is something wrong with your husband?"

"No, but there could be if something isn't done." She was very nervous and said, "I've got to get out of bed."

"Why, you're too sick to do that! Just tell me. What is it you want done?"

Mrs. Pollard hesitated. "I don't know if I should tell you. I'm not supposed to—"

Instantly Leah understood that the problem had to do with Mr. Pollard's trip on the blockade runner. "I know about Mr. Pollard's trip. I haven't said anything."

"Oh, you do!" There was relief in Mrs. Pollard's face. "Then you've got to help me, Leah. Read this!"

45

Leah took the note and looked at the few scrawled lines.

> A Union agent has been uncovered. He will be on board the *Greyhound*. Leaving the harbor, he will signal the Federal gunboats and reveal the position of the ship. *He must be apprehended!*

Leah looked at Mrs. Pollard and exclaimed, "Why, this is awful! Your husband will be captured—and Belle Boyd too."

"We've got to get a message to him. Captain Bier has to know about this—and my husband too."

"Is there anyone we can send?"

"I don't know." Mrs. Pollard seemed confused. She had taken some medicine earlier, and perhaps it had made her thoughts cloudy. Her hands trembled as she ran them across her hair. "Oh, my poor husband—he could wind up in a penitentiary for the rest of the war—and poor Belle, as well!"

Instantly the answer came to Leah. *"I* can take this message to your husband!"

"But it's all the way to Wilmington, North Carolina!"

"A train runs there," Leah reminded her. Mr. Pollard had told her this. "All I have to do is get on the train, ride it to Wilmington, find the ship, and give the message to your husband. Then I can come right back."

"But—but you're only a girl."

Leah's pride was touched. "I can do it! The only problem is leaving you alone for a little while —but Uncle Silas will be here. You tell him that I'll be back as soon as I can."

Leah had to convince Mrs. Pollard, but there seemed to be no other way. She went to her room at once, dressed, and decided to write a quick note to her uncle. When she went back to Mrs. Pollard, she gave her the note, saying, "There may be an early train out—I think there is. I need to get to Wilmington as quick as I can."

Mrs. Pollard held out her arms, and Leah came and took the woman's kiss. "Be so careful, my dear. I wouldn't want anything to happen to you."

"I'll be fine." Leah nodded with a bright smile. "After all, it's just a little trip on a train. I'll be fine!"

5

Desperate Journey

Leah carried a small reticule containing one change of clothes. *I may have to stay overnight,* she thought, *and those trains are awfully dirty.* She walked all the way to the station and found the ticket agent. He seemed surprised to see her so early in the morning.

"What time does the next train go to Wilmington?" she inquired.

"To Wilmington? Well, there's one that comes along at six." He took a watch out of his pocket and stared at it. "Ought to be making up right now. You want a ticket?"

"Yes, I do. How much is it?"

"Three dollars, Confederate."

"Is that one way?"

"Yep. Round-trip will run you five dollars."

As she paid the cash in Confederate notes out of her small purse, the agent looked at her carefully, then said, "You all by yourself?"

"Yes, and I'll be coming back as soon as I can."

"Well, you be careful of them soldiers. This train'll be packed with 'em, all headed down to Wilmington. Some of them is pretty rough, I'm afraid. They'll pester to death a pretty girl like you."

Leah was a little flustered but held her chin up. "I'll be all right," she said. Actually she was rather disturbed but refused to let the agent see that she was troubled.

"Guess you will," the agent said admiringly. "You can set over there, if you want to. Shouldn't be over an hour."

Leah took a seat, and within half an hour the station area was swarming with troops. There must have been at least a hundred of them. By the time the old wood-burning engine pulled its cars up to the depot, she had been the target of many eyes. She was the only young woman in sight; the rest were all officers and enlisted men.

"I guess you can get on now, miss," the agent told her. He winked at a young sergeant who was standing close by, watching Leah. "Sergeant, why don't you see this young lady gets on and gets a seat?"

"Why, sure!" the soldier exclaimed. He was a muscular young man with a fine crop of whiskers of which he seemed very proud, for he stroked them continually. "I'm Sergeant Miller, miss. Can I have your name?"

"Leah Carter."

"Well, now, Miss Leah, you just come with me."

As Sgt. Miller led her to the train, there were whistles and catcalls. "Hey, Sarge, how come you get all the pretty girls?" a tall, lanky soldier carrying a musket said.

"You get back in that line, Private!" Miller said sternly. "I'll take care of this young lady."

Sgt. Miller helped Leah onto the train and carefully escorted her down the aisle, which was already packed with soldiers. She felt terribly embarrassed. Where would she sit?

But Sgt. Miller stopped before two privates. "All right, Cox, you and Rochester just lost your seats."

The two privates stared, then grinned. "Guess you got the best of the argument, Sarge," the smaller one said.

"Take a seat right there by the window, miss," Sgt. Miller said.

When Leah was seated, he said, "Let me have that suitcase. I'll see that it's stored for you so you don't have to hold onto it." He handed the suitcase to one of the privates who had just been evicted. "Cox, take Miss Leah's suitcase out to the baggage compartment." Then he sat down beside her. "I'd better sit here. Not all these fellows are the gentlemen they should be."

"Oh, I'm sure they are." Leah smiled. "They're all soldiers of the Confederacy."

Laughter went over the car, for the soldiers close by were listening avidly.

Actually, Leah turned out to be very grateful to Sgt. Miller. She realized that if he had not plopped himself down beside her, she would have been pestered to death indeed by the attentions of the troops. Most of them looked very young to her, and she wondered if any of them knew Jeff.

"Where's your unit from, Sergeant?"

"We're Third Arkansas. I come from Bald Knob, myself."

"Bald Knob?" Leah stared at the young fellow. "What an odd name."

"Well, it's a nice little town."

"Where is it in Arkansas?"

"Oh, it's about five miles south of Wetwash."

Leah could not help smiling again. "Oh," she said. "Well, that clears it up, of course."

A soldier sitting behind them leaned forward and tapped Miller on the shoulder. "Sarge, this lady will think all of Arkansas's got crazy names like Bald Knob and Wetwash."

Leah turned, and he smiled. He was a handsome boy with blond hair and alert blue eyes. "Not all of Arkansas has funny names like that."

"Where are you from, Private?" Leah asked.

He flushed slightly and said, "Well, actually I'm from Toad Suck Ferry."

A howl of laughter went up, and then Leah had to listen while odd place names in Arkansas were bandied back and forth.

The soldiers had apparently been on a long march to get to the train. Most of them seemed very tired. Soon all were slumped over or curled up in whatever positions they found comfortable, falling asleep almost instantly.

All but Sgt. Miller, that is. He appeared to be fresh and kept Leah entertained for more than an hour with stories about his hometown and his exploits there. He was quite a boastful young man, but pleasant enough.

"I'm glad you were here to take care of me, Sergeant," she said as the train finally pulled into Wilmington. It had been a long, hard trip, and he had seen that she had been well cared for.

Pulling off his cap, he ran his hands through his curly hair, "Well, now, Miss Leah, I wish I could get you to wherever you're going—but I've got to take care of these mavericks here. Good luck to you!"

"I'll think of you, Sergeant Miller." Leah smiled. She took his handshake and watched him turn with a look of regret and hurry over to where his men were forming a line of sorts.

Leah picked up her bag and found her way into the station. She saw it was beginning to grow dark. She had been on the train for hours.

An older man was just closing up the ticket office, and she asked him about the harbor. He waved vaguely. "Why, it's down there, miss. You can't miss it."

But Leah did miss it. She found out that what was just a short way in the station agent's opinion was actually a very long walk. Finally she did find the harbor, but by now it was almost completely dark. Ships were bobbing at anchor, and there was some activity around them.

"Please, can you tell me where I can find the *Greyhound?*" she asked a naval officer.

"The *Greyhound?* Why, sure. Right down there." He hesitated, then said, "It's getting dark. Maybe I'd better show you, miss. You have a husband on board?"

Leah was startled at the question. But it was almost dark, and she was tall for her age. After the shock passed, she smiled, saying, "No, I just have to find a gentleman and give him a message."

"Well, come this way."

The officer led her along the line of waiting ships; then he stopped suddenly and said, "Well, I'll be. You've missed it, miss. There she goes!"

"Oh, I've got to get on that ship! Isn't there any way?"

The officer looked around, then nodded at a

small skiff with a single sail. "I'll see what can be done, miss." He left for a moment.

"If you can afford to pay," he said, returning with two men dressed like fishermen, "these fellows can get you aboard, or so they claim."

"Oh, yes, I'll pay whatever it costs."

The officer nodded and turned to the men. "Are you sure you can catch that ship?"

"I reckon we can," the taller of the two said laconically. "We've done it many a time. She's just creeping around now. Won't be going out for another hour or two to run the blockade."

The officer nodded. "I hope that helps you, miss."

"Thank you so much!" Leah negotiated payment, then said, "I'm ready now."

The shorter of the two lifted his hand and assisted Leah into the small craft. "I'll shove off, Ed," he said. "Set yourself there, miss."

A fair breeze was blowing, and it caught the single sail of the sloop, puffing it out and making it pop. Instantly the small boat moved out onto the waters. As it glided between the ships at anchor, Leah said, "Are you sure that's the *Greyhound?*"

"Certain sure!" the man named Ed said. "I know it well. I know Captain Bier too. Don't worry, miss. We'll get you there."

The *Greyhound* was moving, though very few of her sails were set. Leah could barely see the vessel in the glowering darkness, but the sailors had no trouble. *They must see in the dark like cats,* she thought. "Is that the *Greyhound* where those lights are bobbing?"

"That's it!" the shorter man said.

The tall one suddenly said, "She's picking up speed, Shorty. I guess we'd better get there in a hurry."

"Right! We'll never catch her if she gets her mainsail set."

Leah was terribly nervous, knowing that she had to get the message to Captain Bier and Mr. Pollard. She sat hanging onto her case, and finally the small boat was positioned just behind the large one.

"Ahoy! Passenger for the *Greyhound!*"

"Not taking passengers!" the call came back at once.

Leah lifted her voice. "Please! My name is Leah Carter. I've got an urgent message for Mr. Pollard and Captain Bier."

A silence followed, then finally the call came, "Come aboard!"

The skiff bumped into hull, and Leah stood to her feet.

"Careful, miss," one of the fishermen said.

She did not wait for his helping hand, however, and a sudden gust of wind caught the small skiff. It threw her off balance, and to her horror she felt herself falling. She managed to throw her suitcase backward, but there was no help for it—she hit the water with a splash.

"Man overboard—I mean, *woman* overboard!" the man called Ed cried.

Leah's dress, instantly soaked, began to drag her down, but she was a good swimmer and came up quickly. Lantern lights began to show on board the *Greyhound*, and men's voices called out. She swam as well as she could toward the ship, which lay low in the water.

"There she is! Grab her!"

She touched the hull, and instantly a rope ladder plunked down beside her. A sailor scrambled down it, and she felt a strong arm grasp her.

"Can you climb up, miss?" the sailor said.

"Yes," Leah gasped. "I'm all right. But I need my reticule."

The skiff had pulled close. "Here it is," Ed said. Then he laughed. "That ain't the way folks usually board a ship!"

Leah climbed aboard, feeling like an utter fool. When she was on deck, she pressed the water off her face with her hands. Then suddenly lantern light blinded her.

"What is this?" a voice suddenly demanded.

Then another voice broke in. *"Leah!"*

Leah looked to one side and saw Jeff Majors standing there, gaping at her in amazement.

Leah felt more like a fool than ever. "Hello, Jeff," she whispered. Then she turned and asked, "Are you Captain Bier?"

The captain stared at her, a smile on his face. "Yes, I am."

"I've got a letter for you, but it's in my reticule. It's for Mr. Pollard, really."

"Well, come on down to my cabin," he said. "You got any extra clothes in this bag?" He picked it up.

She said, "Yes, but the letter's the most important. I can wait."

Captain Bier took her arm and led her along the deck. Jeff stood staring, and she could not bear to look at him.

When she was inside the cabin, Bier said, "I'll

send for Mr. Pollard. He's right around the corner, I think."

While waiting, Leah took some of the hot tea that the captain had been brewing on his own little stove. He didn't ask any questions, and they didn't have long to wait.

Mr. Pollard came bursting in. "Leah! What are you doing here?"

"The young lady says she's got a letter for you, John. I reckon it must be important."

Leah pulled the envelope from her bag. "This came for you last night," she said. "I knew you had to have it, so I came as quickly as I could."

Pollard opened the envelope at once. He looked alarmed and read its contents to the captain. "We've got to find this Union agent," he said.

Captain Bier took the message and scanned it himself, then said sharply, "We'll find him, all right —but we'll have to smoke him out. Come along, Miss Leah. I've got a cabin where you can dry out and change clothes."

"Thank you, Captain, but I need to get back."

"Well, I'm afraid that won't be possible," Bier said regretfully. "You'll just have to make the trip to Bermuda with us. We can't go back now."

"To Bermuda? I can't go *there!*"

She thought Mr. Pollard looked disturbed too, but he said, "I'm afraid you'll have to, Leah." He glanced toward shore. "We can't turn around and go back now."

"But what will your wife and my uncle think?"

"They'll just have to wait—or maybe we can send a message through an incoming ship. Anyway, it won't be a long trip," he said comfortingly.

Leah accompanied the captain to a small cabin that had one bunk and one table in it. It was so tiny she had trouble moving around. But she toweled herself down and put on her dry clothes, thinking, *I'm glad I brought a dress. I couldn't wear this wet one all the way to Bermuda.*

Then she remembered Jeff's eyes, staring at her in astonishment. *I wonder what he thought of me getting fished out of the ocean like that?*

6
Trap for a Spy

Leah struggled to make herself presentable as the *Greyhound* moved across the dark waters of the estuary. Her hair presented the greatest problem. It was so long and thick and heavy that she usually washed it on a warm day, then sat outside and let the sun's warmth dry it. Now, however, the best she could do was towel it vigorously, plait it into braids and finally wind it into a coronet on the back of her head.

As soon as she was finished, she went to the door and made her way down the dark deck. There were no stars, and it was a moonless night. She heard the soft slapping of the waves against the side of the ship and was still so blinded from the light of the lantern in her cabin that she could see almost nothing.

Suddenly she bumped into someone and let out a small scream.

"Be quiet!" Someone reached out and steadied her in the darkness.

"Jeff! Is that you?" Leah whispered.

"Yes, it's me. But we've got to be quiet. Those Federal gunboats are just sitting out there listening for us. It's too dark to see anything, but if they hear us, they'll send a rocket over our heads. Then they'll see us."

Leah wanted to say something to Jeff about how sorry she was about their last meeting and the argument that they had had, but his voice sounded stiff, so she said, "What's going to happen now?"

"I don't know. What are you doing on this ship, anyway?"

"I can't tell you. It's not my secret."

At that moment, another soft voice came out of the darkness. "Miss Carter? Are you there?"

"Yes, I am." Leah recognized the voice, and then her eyes adjusted and she saw the form of the captain.

"Are you all right?"

"Oh, yes, I guess a little water never hurt anybody." She peered beyond him. "Is that you, Mr. Pollard?"

"Yes, it is, Leah."

He came forward, and, although she could not see his face well, she knew that he was pleased with her.

"That was a brave thing you did, coming all the way to warn us about this spy."

"Oh, anyone would have done it," Leah protested.

"I'm not sure about that. But in any case, we're forewarned. Now all we've got to do is catch him."

Jeff could no longer keep quiet. "Catch *who?*" he said. "Is there a spy on the ship?"

"Yes, there is, Jeff," Captain Bier said. "And we've got to move fast."

"Do you know who it is?" Leah asked.

"No. He may be one of the crew. We've got some new men, and it's not always easy to be sure of a man's loyalty."

"I don't see how you can even tell where you're going," Leah protested. She stared out into the darkness but could see practically nothing. "How do you know where you are?"

"I don't really—but the pilot, he does." Captain Bier laughed. "I think pilots have cats' eyes. They know every inch of the waters around here. Come on to my cabin. I'll tell you our plan."

After the door was closed and the curtains were drawn, Captain Bier lit the brass lantern that hung beside his small desk. Turning to the others, he said, "We've got to catch this fellow before he has time to move."

"How do you think he'll let the gunboats know where we are?" Mr. Pollard asked.

"I think he'll set off a rocket when we're within range of them. He probably knows these waters pretty well." He chewed on his mustache for a moment, then said, "Most of the other ports have been closed up tight by the blockade. Wilmington's the best."

Jeff said, "But how are we going to know who it is?"

"Well, here's my plan," the captain said. "I've got at least eight men that I *know* are loyal to the Cause, but the new hands—well, I can't say about them. It's going to be hard to find the agent. He could be on the rail or up on deck anywhere, and as soon as he lets that rocket off, every Federal gunboat in this area will be down on us like ducks on a June bug.

"But I know the four of us are safe, and I know those eight of my men are. That gives us twelve. That leaves—let's see, twelve more men not accounted for. Some of them will be in the engine room, so they won't be setting off any rockets. The rest of us will take a man each, and we'll watch him. There'll be only a certain place where the agent can alarm the gunboats. You'd better stay in the cabin, Miss Carter."

"No!" Leah said. "I can see pretty well in the dark once my eyes get accustomed to it. Just let me watch, and then, if I see someone pulling out a rocket, you can believe I'll holler loud enough."

"Good girl!" John Pollard laughed. "Let's let her do it, Cap."

Captain Bier considered, then said, "All right. We'll do it."

The *Greyhound* moved through the darkness, always hugging the shore. Out in the blackness lurked Federal gunboats with cannon big enough to blow them out of the water, and they would have been alerted that a signal would be given by the spy.

Leah had been stationed by Captain Bier up in the stern. He'd said, "You can watch the whole stern from here. If you see a man do anything unusual, just holler. I'll be right across the way on the port side."

"Which side is that, Captain?"

"The left side. Over there." He moved away then to station his reliable men around the deck. When they were in place, he went back to take up his own position, passing by Leah. "The next ten minutes will be crucial," he said. "We're passing through the shallowest area and the narrowest gaps. If the gunboats catch us here, we're done for."

He disappeared into the darkness, and Leah put her back against a bale of cotton and waited. She could hear the propeller churning up the water. Vainly she peered through the darkness. There were a few stars out now, shedding a little light, and a mere sliver of moon, just enough to see by.

On through the dark waves the *Greyhound* glided. Off to one side was solid land, while to the other was nothing but the coastal waters of the Atlantic. Leah's heart was pounding so hard she thought she could hear it. *I hope the spy doesn't hear it!* Actually, she was hoping that the spy would not be in her area. There would be little she could do but call for help.

On and on and on the long, low ship slipped over the black waters. Somehow the pilot did know every inch of the shoreline and clung as close as he could. The larger, heavy gunboats could not come in this close. They had to wait until the pilot saw his chance and made for the deep water between the Federal forces.

Suddenly Leah felt the boat shift beneath her feet and knew they were turning. "We're heading for the deep water," she murmured and grew tense. "If the spy's going to do anything, it'll be right away."

Her eyes were burning, and she blinked furiously, straining to see through the stygian blackness. Then she heard a faint sound and instantly turned her head to the right, straining her eyes even more.

A dark form appeared not ten feet away. It was a man, and he was creeping along the rail!

If I call out too soon and it's not him, it will tip off the real spy, she thought desperately, *but if I wait too long, he'll fire the rocket!*

Taking a chance, she shifted position so that she could get a better view. Her shoes squeaked, and she stopped, her heart in her throat. She thought that the figure also stopped to look around, and she froze solidly to the spot. Finally the dark form turned his back to her.

What to do? Call out or wait? Chance letting the gunboat hear them? She could not decide and in an agony of indecision stood frozen to the deck.

And then she saw the man take something out of his coat and hold it up.

"Captain Bier! Jeff! Mr. Pollard!"

The man whirled toward her with a curse. He was fumbling with an object in his hand.

Leah continued to yell. She ran toward him then, threw herself at him, and pulled at his arm so that something went clattering. He cursed louder and struck at her, his blow catching her on the shoulder and knocking her to the deck.

All of a sudden another dark form sailed out of the darkness and barreled into the man, who grunted and reeled backward. From the opposite side came another figure. Another blow was struck, and suddenly someone lay on the deck.

Leah scrambled to her feet and moved forward cautiously.

"I think we got him, John!"

"Yes, Captain. Here, you—hold still, or I'll break your neck!" Mr. Pollard was a big man, and as Leah came up she saw that the spy was slight and very short. Mr. Pollard had him around the neck with one hand.

"Well, don't kill him, John." Bier laughed quietly. "Bring him on inside. Maybe we can get the truth out of him."

Then he turned to Leah. "You did a good job. I think I'm going to have to put you on my regular crew."

Leah was happy that she had been able to be of help. She followed the two men into the cabin and listened as Captain Bier interrogated the agent.

"I ain't telling you nothing!" the man said. He was rat-faced with scanty gray hair and a pair of beady eyes. "You ain't got no proof!"

"Oh, I don't know. I think that rocket you were about to fire off is all the proof we need. It'll probably get you hanged," Captain Bier said cheerfully.

Fear came to the small man's face, "You can't hang me! It ain't a hanging offense to let off a rocket!"

"It is if you're a spy, and I say that's what you are," Captain Bier said, stern now. "Watch him, John, while I get one of the men to take him below. We've got a place where we can keep him until we get to Bermuda. Then we'll have a trial."

And that was the way it was. The spy was hauled off, kicking and screaming, by two strong sailors who laughed at his feeble efforts.

When they were gone, Jeff suddenly appeared and said, "What happened, Leah? I couldn't see anything."

"Oh, Mr. Pollard and the captain caught the spy."

Captain Bier, standing close by, said, "Well, we couldn't have caught him without your help, Leah. Your uncle's gonna be mighty proud when he hears what you've done."

"My wife'll be proud too," Mr. Pollard said. "She didn't relish having a husband in jail for the rest of the war."

Leah said, "You think I can get on a boat and go back?"

"Not now," Captain Bier pointed out. "The pilot's already got us out in the open sea. Look over there!"

Leah followed his gesture. "What is it?" she asked.

"See that little light there—and there's another one—and there's another one?"

"Yes, what are they?"

"Federal gunboats. They keep on the move all the time. We're just liable to bump into one." He looked regretfully at her. "Sorry about that, but you'll just have to make this trip, Miss Leah. But you and Jeff, you'll have a good time—get to see Bermuda. That's a sight to behold! Kind of a vacation for the two of you."

That gave Jeff a good chance to speak up and say something nice, she thought. But he didn't. He stared at Leah, turned, and walked out of the cabin.

"What's the matter with that young man?" Captain Bier asked. "He's always been pretty cheerful. You reckon he was scared of all this spy stuff?"

"No, Jeff's not afraid of anything," Leah said.

Captain Bier peered at her carefully. "You've known him before, I take it."

"Yes, we were best friends—once."

"Oh, I see. Yes . . . well . . . I've had young daughters of my own. I know how it is . . . well," he said, "it'll be all right. We'll have some pretty weather tomorrow, I think . . . some nice sunshine . . . get to a nice tropical island." He squeezed her arm and winked. "It'll be real romantic. That young man'll come around."

Leah shook her head slowly. "I don't think so, Captain Bier," she whispered.

Leah started to walk away, and the captain looked after her, scratching his head.

"Blamed if it ain't a job and a chore and an aggravation growing up," he muttered, then turned and went back to his duties.

7
On to Bermuda

The *Greyhound* plunged through the blue-green waves with a rolling motion that Leah at first found a little difficult. Finally, though, she acclimated herself to it and took great pleasure standing in the stern and feeling the up-and-down movement.

Captain Bier came by once, stopping long enough to say, "You think you'll make a sailor, missy?"

"Oh, it's so much fun, Captain Bier. I love it! Why, I wouldn't have missed this for anything!"

"Well, I reckon if we hit a hurricane you won't love it quite so much." He grinned at her. "But right now, I'll have to admit it's right pretty."

Leah looked out over the wide expanse of waves. She had never been at sea before, and something about the vast immensity that lay before her pleased her. The blue sky met the green water in a line, but it was difficult to tell just where one ended and the other began. The green of the waves was broken by whitecaps that glittered under the burning sun. There was a salty tang in the air that made her take deep breaths, and she thought, *The captain's teasing me—but it would be nice to be a sailor.*

Later that morning she encountered Belle Boyd walking around the deck. The young Rebel spy had rosy cheeks, and her dark eyes were sparkling with pleasure. "Isn't this marvelous, Leah? I'm so glad we're here. I always liked the sea," she said, joining arms with Leah. "Have you been to sea before?"

Leah stared out over the rolling billows for a moment, then said, "No, this is my first time."

"I made two short trips, but it was stormy both times. But this is so lovely."

The sailors aboard the *Greyhound* had their eyes full that morning. The two attractive young women were the object of every eye. One sailor became so engrossed with watching them that he ran into the rail and almost fell overboard.

Belle and Leah saw this and giggled. Belle whispered, "Wouldn't it be funny if he did fall overboard? I wonder what the captain would say to him?"

The first officer on the *Greyhound*, a young man named Mailer, was clearly enamored of Belle. Belle herself shared this with Leah. "He follows me around like a puppy," she said. "He's rather handsome but too young for me. Why, he can't be over seventeen!" Her eyes crinkled in a grin, and she said, "Now, *you* are more his age."

"I don't think I need any attention out here," Leah said. Then she added quickly, "Besides, Miss Belle, he's so in love with you that he doesn't even see me."

The two young women were invited to eat at Captain Bier's table at dinner, which was served at five o'clock. Leah was amused that Jeff had to serve the meal. He was dressed in a navy jersey and a pair of white pants, and his hair was plastered back.

"How do you like my new cabin boy?" Bier asked jovially.

Jeff flushed to the roots of his hair. Leah knew he hated serving because she was there. Otherwise he would not have minded it at all.

Belle caught his flush of embarrassment and said, "Why, it's you, Mr. Majors. The last time I saw you, you were in the Stonewall Brigade."

"Yes, ma'am, I still am," Jeff muttered, obviously anxious to get away and hide somewhere.

"Well, how does sea life agree with you?" Belle asked. Her eyes cut across to Leah as she added, "I hear you sailors have a girl in every port. Is there anything to that?"

Jeff blinked with astonishment, then wheeled and left the room, indignation on his face.

Captain Bier and Mr. Pollard exchanged glances. Mr. Pollard said, "You ought not to tease the boy, Belle. He's embarrassed."

Belle Boyd smiled cheerfully. "It's good for young men to be embarrassed from time to time. They cause enough embarrassment to young women, don't you agree?"

"I don't know about that," Captain Bier said. "I don't seem to remember being guilty of that too often."

John Pollard scrutinized the young spy, then asked, "What about you, Belle? I heard you've been engaged two or three times already."

Belle did not seem at all troubled by his comment. "Oh, young men like to think that," she said.

"It's not true then?" Captain Bier pressed.

"Oh, not really. I'm just having too much fun to get married now."

Pollard laughed loudly at this. "Oh, you mean after marriage the fun stops? Is that what you're saying?"

"Not for me," Belle said. "When I marry it'll be to a man that will be so exciting that marriage will be a thrill every day."

Bier leaned back and gazed at her rather doubtfully. "That's kind of a romantic idea you got, Miss Boyd. But then, you are a very romantic young lady."

"Oh, utterly romantic!" Belle Boyd smiled. She looked at Leah. "Are you romantic, Leah?"

"I don't know if I am or not. I don't go around reading a lot of syrupy romances."

"Oh, I do," Belle admitted cheerfully. She brushed her dark hair back from her forehead. "I like to read about romance, and I like to attend romantic balls. I think that's what a woman should do. Why, if I—"

"Captain! Captain Bier!"

Bier jerked himself out of his chair as Lieutenant Mailer came in. "We're being pursued by a Federal ship!"

"How close is she?"

"Maybe two miles away but coming on fast!"

Bier left the cabin without pausing to say goodbye.

Leah and the others came out of their chairs and followed after him. Taking their place at the rail, they looked in the direction that the lieutenant was pointing. Sure enough, there was a speck with a curling plume of smoke rising in the sky.

"I hope he's not as fast as we are," Pollard said. "Some of those gunboats are rather fast."

"What will happen if they catch us?" Leah asked quickly.

"It won't be pleasant! But, of course, nothing will happen to you, Leah."

"It will to me, I think," Belle said calmly. "The Federal authorities told me if they ever caught me again, it would be prison for good."

"I hope it won't come to that." Mr. Pollard saw the captain rushing to the wheelhouse and said, "Captain Bier has gone through this before. He'll get us out of it."

Captain Bier stood on deck, staring at the ship, which was growing larger. "Lieutenant, tell the chief I want all he's got!"

"Aye, sir!"

Leah watched the officer disappear, and soon the pitch of the propellers seemed to pick up. She felt the ship lurch under her feet and said to Belle, "We're going faster!"

"I hope so."

For more than an hour the *Greyhound* plunged her prow into the waters, seeming to fly over the waves—but the pursuing vessel didn't fall out of sight.

"She's a fast ship, that one," Bier muttered, his face very sober. "I can't identify her."

"Shall I tell the chief to give us more steam, sir?"

"Yes—tell him again to give us all he's got!"

The lieutenant disappeared but was back in a short time. "He says he's wringing all he can out of her, sir."

"All right."

"Sir—he says we've about run out of the good coal."

"The anthracite?"

This special coal, Leah had been told, burned hotter than most other varieties.

"Yes, sir."

71

"Blast! I knew we'd pay for sailing with that sorry load of inferior coal!"

"Well, it was all we could get, sir."

The lieutenant's words obviously did nothing to ease Captain Bier's fears. He stood with his feet fixed on the deck as if he were a plant growing there, his eyes glued to the warship. When he glanced up at the thick smoke that was pouring out of the *Greyhound*'s stack, he grunted. "Sorry fuel for a man to have to use!"

Jeff had come topside along with most of the hands. He asked a short, chunky man named Charles Crowder, "What's happening, Charles? Why is our smoke so black?"

"'Cause we're having to use a bad kind of coal. Don't burn hot, so we can't get up a full head of steam."

Jeff stared at the Federal gunboat, which was drawing nearer, and felt a touch of fear. *If they catch us—and if they find out I'm in the Confederate army, they'll put me in a prison camp.* The thought was disturbing, and he swallowed hard. "Do you think we can outrun them?"

"Naw, I don't. They got us this time," Crowder said savagely.

"What will they do to you?"

"Aw, nothin', I reckon. But I won't get paid—and this here has been a good ship."

"What about Captain Bier?"

"He'll go to jail—and so will Belle Boyd, I reckon."

Jeff was filled with despair, and when he saw Leah standing with Belle, he wanted to go talk to her. But the wall between them was too high, so he clenched his teeth and prepared for the worst.

Captain Bier said he could now make out the ship that was bearing down on them. "I think she's the *Dominant,*" he grunted.

Lieutenant Mailer blinked. "She's the one who sank the *Southern Star* then."

"Yes, she's a fast one—and that captain is no fool."

Mailer looked up at the sky anxiously. "Maybe we can lose her after dark."

"She'll be up to us before then—" Captain Bier broke off, and an idea seemed to take him.

"What is it, Captain?"

"You know that turpentine we've got on board?"

"Yes, sir?"

"Well, we've got forty barrels of it. Soak some cotton with the stuff and put it in with the coal."

"Why, yes, sir, but—"

"That turpentine will burn hotter than any coal ever mined. I think it'll give us some extra power. Go on—get the crew to working on it."

"Aye, sir!"

Jeff was one of those pressed into action by Lieutenant Mailer. Obeying the frantic orders of the officer, he drew his knife and sliced through the bindings on a bale. After stuffing the fluffy white cotton into a sack, he ran down to the engine room. The pounding of the engine was deafening!

"Douse that cotton with this turpentine!" Mailer shouted.

Jeff began to pour the clear liquid onto the cotton. The pungent fumes of the chemical bit at his eyes and nose, and when he threw a handful of cotton into the firebox, it almost exploded. The heat struck him in the face, and he ducked back.

"Keep it coming!" the chief yelled.

"She might break apart, Chief!" Lieutenant Mailer cried, blinking from the fumes that filled the engine room.

"You let me worry about that, sir! We got to get away from them Yankees!"

Jeff ran back to the deck to get more cotton, and when he looked up he saw that thick gray smoke was now pouring out of the stack. He made the trip back and forth to the engine room so many times he lost count.

Finally, when he staggered up on deck, Lieutenant Mailer took a hard look at his face. "You're beat out, Majors. Take a break."

Jeff stumbled along the deck, sat down, and gasped for breath. He was sick from the fumes of the turpentine, and his face was crimson from the fierce heat of the engine room. He ducked his head and tried to keep from throwing up, feeling about as bad as he'd ever felt in his life.

"Here—let me bathe your face, Jeff."

A coolness touched his neck, and when he looked up he saw that Leah had come with a basin of water. Her eyes were troubled, and as she bathed his face with the cool water, she said, "You've done too much, Jeff."

"Got to get away from that ship!"

"It won't help if you kill yourself," she said firmly. She continued to move the cloth over his face and neck. "You're close to having a heatstroke."

Jeff felt much better as the cool water sluiced over his head and face. The sickness went away, and at last he said, "Thanks, Leah—that's good."

Leah considered him carefully. "Are you all right now, Jeff?"

"Yes—I'm better." He got to his feet and discovered that his legs were weak. "Guess I did get too hot."

"I got overheated once—when we were picking cotton. Do you remember that?"

"Sure do. We must have been no more than nine years old."

"I was eight—and when you saw how red my face was you dragged me to the creek and put me in it."

"Seems like a long time ago," Jeff murmured. He thought of that day and added, "You got pretty mad at me for dumping you into the creek."

"Yes, but afterwards I knew it was the right thing to do." She looked into his eyes and said softly, "We had some fine times, didn't we?"

"Yes, we did." Jeff wanted to say more, but his pride was still stiff. He tried to bring himself to say he was sorry for all that had happened.

And perhaps he would have found a way to say it, but at that moment Captain Bier yelled, "She's getting close! Lieutenant—tell the chief to add coal dust to the firebox!"

"Coal dust?"

"That's what I said! Do I have to give every order twice?"

Lieutenant Mailer swallowed hard and ran to the ladder.

Leah and Jeff were close enough to the captain to hear him muttering under his breath.

"What would he want to throw coal dust into the fire for?" Jeff wondered.

75

"I can't imagine," Leah said, sounding mystified. "But he's a smart man. I'll bet he's got something in his mind."

"It's almost dark." Jeff looked up at the sky. "If we can just stay out of range for another hour, it'll be dark, and we can sneak away."

Soon not only Jeff and Leah but the crew discovered why the captain had given such a strange order.

John Pollard was standing beside Jeff and Leah. Looking up at the stack, he exclaimed, "Look at that! I've never seen such thick smoke!"

It was a thick, oily smoke that didn't rise but instead fell toward the sea. Within a short time the *Greyhound* had laid down a smoke screen that swallowed up the Federal gunboat.

"She'll never find us in that mess!" Jeff cried out. "And it's getting dark—I think we've made it!"

He proved to be correct, for the billows of black smoke and the falling darkness swallowed up both ships—which was exactly what Captain Bier had planned!

After the excitement of the chase, Belle Boyd said, "Come on down to my cabin, Leah. I'm not sleepy yet—we can talk."

"All right."

Leah accompanied Belle to her cabin, and they sat talking for a long time. Leah had already discovered that Belle loved to speak of her exploits, and once she smiled and said, "You ought to go on the stage, Miss Belle."

"I've thought of that," Belle said seriously. "A lot of people go on the circuit, telling of their adventures. I might bill myself as 'The Lily of the

Shenandoah.' That's one of the names they call me, you know."

"Yes, I know."

"Or maybe just 'The Rebel Spy.'" She stood and took a dramatic position, reciting with theatrical gestures, "And there I was, in the middle of the Battle of Bull Run with all of the weight of winning the battle on my shoulders. I had to get through to the Confederate forces . . ."

She turned around twice, bowed, and then laughed at herself. "How was that?" she asked. "Do you think I could make a living on the stage?"

"I think you could." Leah listened until Belle finally grew quiet, then said, "Were you serious about what you said to the captain?"

"About what, Leah?"

"About marriage."

"Oh, I was just talking. I don't even remember what I said now."

"You said you had to have a romantic courtship and then romance afterwards."

"Well, I would like that. What woman wouldn't?"

"I hear about a lot of romantic courtships, but I don't know about afterwards. Marriage must be especially hard in these times."

Belle Boyd leaned back. She picked up a perfume bottle from the table, took the top off, smelled it, then smiled. "I'd like to find a man that'd sweep me off my feet," she said. "Plenty of them have tried, but none has made it so far."

"Well, one of them will some day, I'm pretty sure."

Leah went to her own cabin then and went to bed. As the ship rose and fell with the waves, she thought about Belle Boyd's desire for a romantic courtship. She rolled over thinking, *That would be nice, but I don't know if it's what I want or not. I'd just like a good, solid man who wouldn't change all the time and would take care of me. Marriage, I think, is more than moonlight and poetry and the stuff that Belle likes.*

8
A Birthday Party

On her second afternoon on the ship, Leah made her way to the galley, where she found James Austin, the cook, preparing the evening meal. She had been friendly with the man and now said, "Mr. Austin, I'd like to do something."

"What's that, Miss Leah?" he asked cheerfully. He was a short man with thinning red hair and china-blue eyes, and there was always a smear of flour on his face.

"Well, it's Miss Belle's birthday, and I'd like to make her a cake if I wouldn't be in the way too much."

"So! You don't tell me! Well, I think we can find enough to put a cake together. Maybe not as fancy as you'd make at home, but we can do the best we can. I think it'd be a shame if we didn't give the Rebel Spy a birthday party."

Leah was pleased that he liked her suggestion. "I can make it, if I won't be in the way."

"Not a bit of it! We'll work on it together. I reckon the two of us can do a bang-up job." He lifted his voice and said, "Jeff!"

Leah turned quickly and saw Jeff come through the door.

When he saw her, he nodded briefly. "Hello," he mumbled.

"Hello, Jeff."

Austin said, "We're going to make a cake for Miss Belle. Move all this stuff over here, and I'll get Miss Leah started on it. You know how to make cakes, don't you, Miss Leah?"

"Oh, yes, I do." Leah expected Jeff to say something about how good a cook she was, but he ignored her glance and went on about clearing the table.

She discovered that all the ingredients for a cake were in the small, well-equipped larder, and soon she had the batter ready and poured it into the pan that Austin gave her.

Popping it into the oven, she said, "I hope it doesn't bake too fast. I never know exactly how my cakes are going to come out."

"Oh, it'll be good. I know a lot about cooks, and you're a good one. I watched you real close," Austin said with a grin. "Miss Belle'll be plumb surprised. Well, nothing to do now. Why don't you two take a stroll around deck?"

Jeff blinked, then said abruptly, "Well, I guess I've got to go get the captain's clothes pressed." He turned and sullenly walked away.

Austin seemed surprised, but he winked at Leah. "That sure is a strange young fellow. When I was his age, if I'd of had a chance to walk a pretty girl home from a dance or to church, you wouldn't have caught me turning it down."

Leah said nothing, but her feelings were hurt. *Why'd he have to be so mean? I thought after I helped him when he got too hot, we'd make up*, she thought. *He's just not like the old Jeff. If that's what growing up is, I think he should have stayed what he was!*

The birthday party proved to be an astounding success. The captain came. Mr. Pollard was there. Lieutenant Mailer dazzled them all with a sparkling fresh uniform and his mustache waxed until it had needle points.

Belle was delighted at the attention. There were no gifts, but they all sang "Happy Birthday," and when she tasted the cake she said, "Why, Captain, you've got a fine cook! My compliments to him."

"Austin had little to do with this," the captain said. "This is Miss Leah's baking."

"Is that so? My, what a fine cook you are, Leah!" Belle smiled. She took another bite and rolled her eyes. "This is the best birthday cake I've ever had in my life!"

"I think we ought to have some entertainment," the captain said. "John, you used to be a pretty fair tenor. You suppose we might make a quartet—you and me, Miss Belle and Miss Leah?"

Leah protested, but Belle urged her, and they soon found that they knew all the words to "Aura Lea." It was a favorite all over the South, and after getting a pitch from the captain, they sang the song:

> "When the blackbird in the spring
> On the willow tree
> Sat and rocked I heard him sing,
> Aura Lea, Aura Lea,
> Maid of golden hair,
> Sunshine came along with thee,
> Swallows in the air."

They sang the chorus:

> "Aura Lea, Aura Lea,
> Maid of golden hair,
> Sunshine came along with thee,
> And swallows in the air."

Then they sang four more verses:

"In thy blush the rose was born,
Music when you spake,
Through thine azure eyes the morn,
Sparkling seemed to break.
Aura Lea, Aura Lea,
Birds of crimson wing
Never song have sung to me
As in that sweet spring.

"Aura Lea! The bird may flee,
The willow's golden hair
Swing through winter fitfully,
On the stormy air,
Yet if thy blue eyes I see,
Gloom will soon depart;
For to me, sweet Aura Lea,
Is sunshine through the heart.

"When the mistletoe was green,
Midst the winter's snows,
Sunshine in thy face was seen,
Kissing lips of rose.
Aura Lea, Aura Lea,
Take my golden ring;
Love and light return with thee,
And swallows in the spring."

They sang for two hours—"Dixie," "Lorena," "The Wearing of the Gray," and many others.

After the party, Belle gave Leah a kiss. "That was very thoughtful of you, Leah. I know it was your idea. No one else knew it was my birthday."

"Oh, it was fun making the cake."

"When we get to Bermuda, I'll take you out and buy you a meal at a fine restaurant. They say there's all sorts of things to do there."

As it happened, however, Leah never got the meal that Belle Boyd promised her. Later she thought about how strange it was: life was so uncertain that one could never be sure of even such a simple thing as a meal.

9

The USS *Connecticut*

Leah was awakened by shouting on the deck. She started out of a sound sleep, confused by the pounding of feet running outside her cabin. Sitting up straight, she rubbed her eyes and shook her head. Then she heard the captain's voice yelling commands.

Quickly she jumped out of bed and hastily dressed. Stepping outside, she saw that the morning was just beginning to dawn. She was joined at the ship's rail by Belle, who had evidently dressed as hurriedly as she herself. They stared at each other for a moment, then looked over the sea.

"What is it?" Leah asked.

"Another Federal warship—just exactly what we didn't need!" Belle nodded toward the east.

There, outlined against the gray, milky-looking sky, was the dreaded form of an approaching warship. It had been two days since the *Greyhound* had escaped the first Union ship; now here was another!

"We'll outrun them," Leah said confidently. "The captain knows how to dodge them. We'll slip away, and they'll never catch us!" Actually she was not sure of this, but she spoke as if she were.

Apparently Captain Bier was not sure. He had a worried look on his face. As Lieutenant Mailer stood beside him, he lifted his spyglass and peered through it.

"What is it, Captain? Can you make 'er out?" the lieutenant asked anxiously.

"I think it isn't good news for us." He would say no more about the warship but added, "Have the hands served breakfast. It may be a long chase, and I want the men in good shape."

He began to pace back and forth on the deck, pausing from time to time to look at the horizon. There was a stiffness in his back and a frown on his face.

By now almost all hands were topside, staring at the enemy ship.

John Pollard approached Bier, saying, "What is it, Captain?"

"Federal warship, and a fast one, I'm thinking."

Pollard's brow wrinkled. "They caught us at a bad time. If it was almost dark, we might slip away. Now, we'll just have to outrun her."

"And I'm not sure we can do that," Captain Bier said calmly. "We're out of the better grade of coal—and I don't think we can use the turpentine trick again." He lifted the spyglass and stared at the approaching ship. "I hope I'm wrong, but that may be the USS *Connecticut.*"

"You know her, Captain?"

Captain Bier lowered the glass, folded it up, and held it at his side. "I know her," he said. "She's the fastest ship the Federals have."

"Not faster than the *Greyhound?*"

Captain Bier gave Pollard a direct look. "Aye, I'm afraid she is, John. And she's heavily armed. We're in for it this time."

Belle and Mr. Pollard met at the bow.

"We'd better make plans, Belle," Pollard said, a worried look on his face. "I don't think we've got much of a chance this time."

"The only plan I have is to get rid of the papers President Davis entrusted to me. If they found those, we'd be in real trouble."

"You know it'll probably be prison for you—perhaps for me, as well," Mr. Pollard said.

"Not for you. They'd never dare do that."

"For you it's worse."

"I know. They've been looking for an excuse to lock me up again." But Belle tossed her head, a rebellious light in her eyes. She stared at the warship, which was drawing closer by the moment. "Don't worry about me, John. I'll be all right."

The *Greyhound* was a three-masted, propeller steamer of four hundred tons. She was painted lead gray with a red streak along her hull. She was a shallow-draft ship, which meant that she could hug the shoreline closer than the Yankee gunboats—but that also meant she was not as fast in open water. The approaching ship was new and obviously very fast.

Captain Bier looked tense. He glanced up at the masts, then at the enemy vessel. "We'll put up the sails, Lieutenant," he said sharply. "We're going to need all the leverage we can get. Put every square inch of canvas on!"

The *Greyhound*, like many other ships of her time, was caught between the age of sail and the age of steam. Many shipowners—and captains as well—did not entirely trust the new steam engines. They were in fact sometimes unreliable, and it was considered insurance to be able to catch the winds if the engines failed.

Soon the sails were billowing out overhead, and Leah stared at them, asking, "Captain, do you think that'll be enough?"

"I don't know, Leah—it's doubtful."

Half an hour later, the cruiser had pulled within firing range. A thin, white curl of smoke rose high in the air as the *Connecticut* turned and launched a broadside. Leah heard a hissing, and then in the sea a few yards from the *Greyhound* a geyser spouted up, along with an explosion underwater.

"That's too close!"

Leah turned to see Jeff. His face was anxious, and he gripped the rail tightly.

"Jeff, don't let the officers on that ship find out you're in the Confederate army!"

"I already thought of that. But most of the crew know it—some of them, anyway."

"We've got to tell them to keep it to themselves."

Jeff stared at her. "How can we do that?"

"We'll just go to them and tell them. Come on!"

Leah whirled, and for the next half hour the pair moved along the upper and lower decks, speaking to the hands. All agreed, most of them saying, "Right! None of their business, anyway!"

Finally they had spoken to all the crew, and Jeff said awkwardly, "Thanks, Leah. I'd never have thought of that." He hesitated, then said, "I've been a real grouch lately. Never did thank you proper for sponging me down when I got so hot."

Leah flushed. "Oh, that was nothing!"

"It was something—and I won't forget it—" He seemed about to say more, but at that instant a cannonball struck the sail over their heads, breaking the spar. Jeff grabbed Leah and shoved her to one side. They fell to the deck as canvas and rigging came crashing down. And then the heavy sail covered them.

"Leah—are you all right?" Jeff cried.

"Yes—how about you?"

Jeff sighed with relief. "I'm OK—but let's get out from under this thing. Some more rigging might fall on us."

Scrambling out from under the canvas, Leah could hear the cruiser firing rapidly.

"We can't stand that!" Jeff said and clenched his teeth. Then he ran toward the ladder to the galley.

The *Connecticut* sent volley after volley at the *Greyhound,* some shells bursting overhead and some falling short.

Captain Bier stood rigidly on deck, glancing at the compass and yelling orders. The shot and shell fell thick and fast near the *Greyhound,* and the captain turned to Belle, who was standing close by. "If it wasn't for you, I'd burn the ship. Then at least the Yankees wouldn't get the cargo."

Belle answered at once, "Do what you must, Captain. Don't think about me!"

The *Connecticut* was now less than half a mile away.

"It's too late to burn her now," Captain Bier said. "We'll have to surrender." At his command, the *Greyhound* swung around, and Lieutenant Mailer raised a white flag.

But five minutes later as the cruiser closed, a shell hurtled close overhead.

"The cowards!" Bier shouted. "Do they mean to fire on a ship that's surrendered?"

The cruiser came alongside, and a loud voice called, "We are coming aboard. Have all your men throw down their arms!"

Belle ran down the deck and disappeared into her cabin.

Surprised, Leah watched her go. She herself stayed in place on the deck as the warship came ever closer.

Then Belle was out again, carrying a leather case.

"What is it, Belle?" Leah asked.

"Papers from President Davis to the ministers in England." She looked around. "I've got to weigh this down and throw it overboard. If they found it, Leah, I'd go to prison for sure—or maybe even be hanged."

"I'll get something," Leah said. She ran down to the galley, where she found Jeff standing at the door, watching. "Let me by, Jeff!" she demanded and sailed past the astonished boy.

Inside the galley, she found what she was looking for—the long-handled iron skillet that Austin used for frying fish. Grabbing it up, she took an apron at the same time. She brushed past Jeff again and climbed again to the top deck.

"Here! This will do, Belle," she said. She tied one end of the apron to the hole in the handle of the frying pan while Belle tied the other end to the handle of the case.

Then, lifting the case high, Belle threw it overboard. It sank at once, and Belle drew a deep sigh of relief. "Now, at least," she said, "they won't have that to use as evidence against me."

10

A Gallant Officer

Captain Bier watched with regret as two sailors rolled a keg containing $30,000 in gold over the side of the *Greyhound*, but he knew he could not allow it to fall into the hands of the enemy.

Then the captain of the *Connecticut* came aboard and recognized Captain Bier at once.

Bier saluted him, saying, "We meet again, Captain Almy."

Captain Almy seemed somewhat shocked to see Bier. He was a tall man with muttonchop whiskers and cold blue eyes. "I'm sorry it's come to this, Bier," he said.

"So am I," Captain Bier said sardonically. "I surrender the ship to you, sir."

"If we could go to your cabin, I'd like to make some records of this transaction."

"Of course, Captain."

The two men went below, and when they had spoken for some time of the details of the surrender, Captain Almy leaned back in his chair and shook his head. "Never thought it would come to this, Bier."

"There's risk in running the blockade. I won for a long time—and now I've lost."

"You've never cried over your losses—I remember that."

"No point, is there?"

Captain Almy appeared troubled. "You should have joined the U.S. Navy. You'd have been high in the service by now."

"We all make our choices, sir."

"But the Confederacy was doomed from the start!"

"A man must stand for what he believes."

"Even if what he believes is wrong?"

"Slavery is wrong. I know that as well as any man."

"Then why didn't you fight for our side?"

Bier studied Almy carefully. "Suppose your family took a wrong position, sir. Then suppose that you were asked to fight against them. Would you do it?"

Captain Almy sat in his chair, silent and thinking. He finally shook his head. "I can't say that I would. But it's not quite the same thing."

"It's the way I see it, sir. I can't fight against my neighbors and my family."

Almy saw that there was no fear—and no regret—in Captain Bier. *I wish he were on our side*, he thought ruefully. *We need men like him.*

As the two captains were talking below, a short officer came to where Belle stood and grinned nastily. "I was the one that fired that last shot that came so close to you," he said proudly.

Belle gave him a cold glance. "I hope you're proud of yourself for firing on a ship that had already surrendered."

"None of that," he said. "I'm Ensign Swasey, and I'll be in command of the prize crew. You mind your manners, or I'll have you locked in irons."

"I believe you, sir," she said in a frigid manner. "I believe you're just the kind of man who would do such a thing."

Swasey's face reddened, and he turned away, bawling orders.

Leah and Belle went to stand beside Mr. Pollard as the Federal sailors came pouring onto the deck of the *Greyhound*.

Swasey yelled, "Go below, men!" He grinned at Captain Bier and shouted another order. "If you see anything you need, take it."

Belle said, "We'd better get to our cabins. I don't want them pawing through my things!"

"I don't have any things for them to paw through," Leah said, "but I'll go with you."

The girls went below. They saw that sailors had already burst into some of the cabins and were rifling their contents, taking what they pleased.

"Why, they're nothing but pirates!" Belle exclaimed angrily when they stood in her cabin.

A sailor heard her and came to the door, a big man with a red complexion. He leered at her, saying, "Watch your speech, dearie, or I may have to search you for hidden papers."

Belle said, "You wouldn't dare touch me!"

"Wouldn't I, now?" The sailor stepped into the cabin and reached for Belle.

She slapped him across the face.

The sailor stood there, stunned that a woman would do such a thing. He growled, "I'll teach you a lesson—"

"I'll go report to his captain," Leah said quickly. "I'm sure he'd like to know how his sailors are behaving." She dashed out of the cabin, avoiding the sailor, who made a wild grab for her.

Leah scrambled up the ladder and saw at once that the captain of the *Connecticut* had boarded. She ran across the deck. "Captain! Your men are stealing things from our cabin, and one of them is forcing himself on a young lady!"

Captain Almy looked in some confusion at the young girl who had planted herself in his way. In his scratchy voice he said, "What's that you say?"

The girl repeated her news and said, "It was my understanding that officers of Federal warships were gentlemen. Is that not so, Captain?"

"Certainly!" Almy turned to his aide. "Lieutenant, go below. See that the men behave themselves."

"Aye, sir!"

"Thank you, Captain," the girl said gratefully.

"Well—*harumph!* The men sometimes get carried away." He stared at her and said, "What are *you* doing on this ship? Are you a Southern girl?"

"My brother's in the Union army, and my father's a sutler following the Army of the Potomac."

"Then what are you doing on a blockade runner?"

"It's a long story, Captain. I came to Virginia originally to visit my uncle who is ill—"

"Well, I don't have time to hear this. The best thing for you, young lady, is to get yourself out of the South as quick as you can!"

Almy stomped across the deck to the Rebel captain. "Well, Captain Bier, I'm making a prize ship of the *Greyhound*. I suppose you expected that."

"Yes, I did. The victory's yours, Captain Almy." There was sadness in Bier's voice, and he ran his hand over the rail in a loving fashion. "She's a good ship."

Almy said. "Be good for us keeping the blockade. I think she's fast enough to catch some of your other blasted blockade runners!"

"I could kill that Ensign Swasey."

Belle Boyd had a fiery temper. Walking back and forth in the narrow confines of her cabin, she stepped on Leah's foot without even knowing it. It was painful but Leah said nothing, merely pulling her foot back.

"He's not very pleasant," she agreed.

They had both been insulted by the squat ensign who was in charge of the ship. He had been put aboard with the prize crew, and soon they were sailing toward Boston where the *Greyhound* would be converted, they understood, to a blockading warship.

"I can't believe that such a beast would be wearing the uniform of an officer," Belle fumed. She plunked herself down on the bunk and wrung her hands. "I hate that man! He's let his sailors do practically anything they want. They've been rude and insulting and made crude suggestions." She looked at Leah. "To you too, I suppose?"

Leah had suffered some of the same indignities, but she didn't add anything to what Belle was saying. It seemed to her that complaining was useless.

Belle fussed and fretted and argued, but of course there was nothing Leah could do but agree with her.

"Well, come along. It's time for lunch. If we get any lunch!" Belle said.

"I suppose we'll have to eat with the Union officers."

"Yes, I'm sure we will. I hope Swasey's table manners are better than the rest of his manners," Belle bristled.

They left the cabin and were on their way to the dining room when the object of Belle's distaste suddenly stepped out into the passageway.

"Well, Miss Boyd," he said, smiling unpleasantly, "I suppose your spying days are over."

"Let me pass, please."

But as Belle attempted to get by, Swasey blocked her way. "You should have been locked up for good a long time ago, but I'm going to see to it that it happens now. I have some friends in Washington that will do anything I ask them to do."

Once again Belle tried to walk by him.

This time Swasey grabbed her arm. "Not so fast! I'm not through talking yet!"

Belle pulled away from him furiously, saying, "Let me go!"

"Let the lady go, Ensign."

Swasey wheeled quickly, and the girls turned to see a tall young officer who had come out of a cabin. He was well built, had long dark hair, auburn in color, and the bluest eyes that Leah had ever seen.

"You must be Miss Boyd and Miss Carter."

"Yes, I am Belle Boyd." She seemed ready to let some of her rage boil over on this officer, but she had no time.

Swasey said, "You stay out of this, Hardinge! I'm in charge of this ship—or will be as soon as the captain leaves."

"There's been a change in plans, I'm afraid, Ensign." The ensign named Hardinge turned his steady eyes on the shorter man. "Captain Almy has put me in charge of the prize crew. You'll be under my command."

"Why, he can't—he can't do that!"

"Why don't you go tell him that, Ensign Swasey?" Hardinge said, a smile turning up the corners of his lips. "I'm sure he'd welcome hearing from one of his officers that he can't do something."

Swasey puffed his cheeks out and glared at Belle. "We'll see about this!" he rasped and disappeared into the cabin.

Removing his hat, the tall, dark ensign said, "My name is Sam Hardinge, ladies, and I've just spoken the truth to Ensign Swasey."

"He's been quite unbearable," Belle said. However, it seemed to Leah that she was mollified by the courtesy and quiet bearing of the young Union sailor.

"I apologize, Miss Belle," Hardinge avowed. "I'll see to it that you're not offered any further indignities by the ensign." He smiled then.

He looks like an actor, Leah thought suddenly. *He's better looking than any of the other sailors I've seen.*

Hardinge said quickly, "I must begin by telling you how much I respect your efforts for your country, Miss Boyd."

Belle Boyd was accustomed to admiration from the young men of the Confederacy. However, she was also accustomed to hatred from those who were on the opposite side. Young Hardinge's statement obviously took her completely off guard. She colored and stammered as she rarely did before any man. "Why . . . why . . . well, I didn't expect—"

"You didn't expect a Yankee to say such a thing?" Sam Hardinge laughed. "I think you'd find many from the North who respect your courage, Miss Belle. We may not agree with your convictions, but who could help admiring such devotion to a cause?"

"Why, thank you, Ensign." Belle's lips had softened, and she turned to Leah, saying, "Now, this is the way an officer should be." Turning back to Hardinge, she said, "Sir, you are polite and gentlemanly enough to be a member of the Confederate navy or army."

"A high compliment, indeed, coming from you, Miss Belle." Hardinge smiled and then extended his arm. "May I escort you to dinner? I've saved a place at the captain's table. And for you too, Miss Leah."

"Well, of course, that would be very nice."

Leah followed the pair in, and she was amused all through the meal at how the handsome young ensign had captured Belle's attention. *She's accustomed to men admiring her, but this one has really taken her off guard,* Leah thought.

She leaned over and whispered to Mr. Pollard, who was sitting next to her, "What do you think of Belle's attitude toward Ensign Hardinge?"

Pollard whispered back, "She's used to having men admire her, but I've never seen her quite so taken with a young man. It's a shame he's a Yankee, or I'd think she might fall in love with him."

Leah studied Belle, whose attention was totally fixed on Ensign Hardinge, taking in his every word. "Well, Yankee or not, I think Belle'd better watch out. She sure is giving him some sweet looks!"

97

11

Love Is a Funny Thing

Jeff threw his knife on the floor and stood up, his face defiant. "I'm not going to peel another potato, Austin!" he declared.

The cook looked up from where he was cleaning a skillet. His face showed surprise. "What do you mean, you're not going to peel any more potatoes?"

"I mean I didn't come on this trip to feed Yankee sailors!" Jeff protested.

"No more did I," Austin said. He shrugged his heavy shoulders. "None of us thought we'd be in the hands of the Yankees. But that's the way it goes with running the blockade. That's a chance we all take."

"Well, I'm not going to serve them anymore," Jeff snapped. "They can peel their own potatoes!"

"I don't think that'll answer, lad," Austin said quietly. He stared at the boy with some compassion. "The potatoes are going to feed our own men as well as the Yankees, so just sit down there and keep on peeling."

Jeff reluctantly retrieved the knife, sat down, and picked up a potato. He started a peeling and watched it uncurl, muttering bitterly, "I wish this was that Ensign Swasey's head. Now that's what I'd like to peel!"

"He *is* a varmint now, ain't he?"

"I keep hoping he'll fall overboard—but he'd probably poison all the fish if he did."

Austin chuckled deep in his chest. "Well, he ain't been bothering the young ladies much, not since that Ensign Hardinge put the skids under him. Now there's a pretty nice young fellow!"

"He's not bad," Jeff admitted grudgingly, "but he's a Yankee all the same."

Jeff peeled potatoes until the chore was done, then said, "I'm going up and take a break. I can't help feeling funny down here all the time. It makes me feel peculiar all cooped up below deck."

Austin gave him a look of amusement. "You wouldn't make a good sailor then, because a lot of our lives are spent down below, especially cooks."

"No, I'll be glad to get back to the army. This hasn't turned out like I thought it would."

Jeff climbed to the deck and drifted back toward the stern. Some Yankee sailors were patrolling with their pistols in their belts, but there was little chance that anyone would try to escape. Leaning on the rail, he watched the water boil behind the *Greyhound*, churned to a white froth by the propeller. They were making good time, but that did not please him at all. Then he heard someone call his name.

He turned quickly and found Leah standing and watching him. "Oh," he said lamely, then added, "hello, Leah."

"Hello, Jeff."

He waited for her to say more, and when she did not, he shifted his feet uncomfortably. He had a strange feeling about Leah. Somehow he had convinced himself that their argument was all her fault. More than once he realized this was foolish, but the mind has a funny way of doing things like that. "How's Miss Belle?" he finally asked, not expecting an answer but just to make conversation.

Leah came over and stood at the rail, looking down at the water. "She's all right—she and Ensign Hardinge are walking together up in the bow."

"Seems to me like she's spending a lot of time with that Yankee."

"She is. I don't think I've ever seen anybody quite like him."

"Well, he's nice-looking, all right," Jeff admitted grudgingly, "but he's still a Yankee."

"She knows that. Miss Belle doesn't usually mistake Yankees for Confederates." At once Leah appeared sorry she had spoken so sharply. "I'm sorry. I don't know what's wrong with me, talking like that."

Jeff bit his lip and tried to find a way to say what was inside him, but he could only say lamely under his breath, "Well, I guess we've all been under a strain."

"What do you think will happen to us, Jeff?"

"I don't imagine they'll put us in jail. They might if they knew I was in the Confederate army —but you took care of that."

"It wasn't just me."

"Sure it was. You thought of it."

She seemed pleased with his gratitude. "Well, anyway, I'm glad we did it. You don't need to be in a prison. They're bad. Ezra almost died in one."

It suddenly pleased Jeff that she was worried about him, and he was about to say he was sorry. But again he somehow had trouble getting the words out and just said gruffly, "Well, I guess I'd better go back—got work to do." As he walked away, he thought glumly, *Why do I have to act like such a mule around Leah? I'm all mixed up.*

Belle was brushing her dark hair when a tap came at her cabin door. "Who is it?" she called out.

"Ensign Hardinge!"

"Oh!" She took a look at herself in the mirror, smoothed her hair, then put down the brush and rose to her feet.

She opened the door, smiling. "Yes, Ensign Hardinge?"

"I brought some special coffee on board from the *Connecticut*. Been saving it for a special occasion. Would you come and have a cup with me, Miss Belle?"

"Why, I'd be delighted to, Ensign."

As she stepped outside, Hardinge said, "Do you think you could ever come to call me something besides *Ensign?* I feel like saluting you every time you say that. Perhaps Sam?"

Belle laughed. "I don't think that would be very appropriate. After all, I'm your prisoner. You shouldn't call your jailer by his first name."

Hardinge smiled down at her. He seemed completely captivated by her. Perhaps he had been ready to be captivated. She knew he would have read everything printed about the Rebel Spy. Perhaps he had expected to find her less than the accounts that he had read but had found that they had understated her charms.

"Well, perhaps when we're alone, then. Just once in a while. It would make me feel more human."

"I'll think about it, Ensign." Belle smiled up at him.

They entered the dining room, and she found that Hardinge had one of the tables set with a white cloth. There were small cakes on a silver tray, and a sailor dressed in white was standing there with hot coffee.

Hardinge seated her, and, after the sailor had poured the coffee and left, she picked up hers and sipped it. "Oh, this is heavenly," she said. "I love coffee."

"So do I," Sam Hardinge said. He took one of the cakes and tasted it. "I love cakes too. If I ate all I wanted, I'd probably weigh three hundred pounds."

Belle did not think this was likely. He was better built than any man she had ever seen, with a neat, tidy waist, broad shoulders, and a deep chest. Looking at him, she thought, *He's almost too pretty to be a man. Still, he's virile enough for all of that!*

She sat there with him happily, eating cakes and enjoying the coffee.

Finally Hardinge said, "What will you do after the war is over, Belle—if I may call you that here in private?"

"I suppose that will be all right—Sam." She favored him with a smile. Then she thought of his question. "I don't know. I don't suppose many of us in the South can think that far ahead. It's a matter of living day by day."

Hardinge dropped his head and stared into his coffee cup. "I know your people have suffered dreadfully—more than the people in the North. And I'm sorry."

His simplicity and honesty touched her. Without thinking, she reached over and put her hand on his. "I know that comes from your heart," she murmured. "You're a very strange man, Sam Hardinge. Most Yankees are not so thoughtful."

"Most are. We're all caught in this."

Hardinge had to be very much aware of her firm, warm hand on his.

She removed it to pick up her cup.

"Are you engaged, Belle?" he asked suddenly.

"Not at the moment," she said demurely.

Hardinge grinned again, which made him look very young—and very handsome too. "So right now you're between fiancés, so to speak?"

He had a wit that she liked. She enjoyed being teased and had found out that Hardinge could do it tastefully. "Yes, you might say that. Sometimes I've let myself get engaged to Union officers," she said, "so that I could find out what their troops were doing."

"Well—" Hardinge pretended to think this over "—I don't have any troop movements to report, but I'd be perfectly willing to let you try out your charm on me. I think it would be successful. Come now, try to get my secrets!"

Belle suddenly realized, *I'm flirting with this man, and he's right—he doesn't have any information to give me. The only Yankees I've flirted with are those that I wanted something out of. But Sam is different!*

Finally Belle realized with a start how long they had been talking. "My gracious!" she said. "I don't believe this ship needs you at all for a commander. We've been here an hour, and it's still going along. I thought you had to steer this ship?"

"Be hard to miss Boston." Hardinge made a face. He stood to his feet, and when she rose he said quietly, "I wish you didn't have to go to Boston. I

103

know it will be unpleasant for you there, and I'm sorry."

"That's the second time you've said that—John —that you're sorry. I can't believe that all Yankees treat their prisoners in such a kindly and compassionate manner."

Suddenly Hardinge took her hand and raised it to his lips. "How could I be less than gentle to a woman with a spirit and a beauty such as yours?"

He released her hand and stepped back, adding, "I hope I haven't offended you."

Belle was flustered. She had romanced enough officers so that a kiss on her hand came as no shocking thing. Still, there was something in his manner that she liked tremendously.

"How gallant you are, sir," she whispered, then turned and left the dining room.

"I tell you, Hardinge, you've got to stop it!" Swasey's face was red. His back was erect, and there was anger in his eyes.

"Stop what, Swasey?"

"Don't beat around the bush. You know what I mean—romancing that Rebel spy!"

Hardinge turned to look at him. "You tend to your duties, Mr. Swasey, and I'll appreciate it."

"You're setting a bad example before the men."

"Do you want to charge me with any misconduct?"

"Well . . . not directly . . . but you ought to have better sense. You know what she is."

"What does that mean—I 'know what she is'?"

"I mean, she's been in prison. She's a spy. You know she is—you've read about her."

"Ensign Swasey, that's the end of this conversation! Get about your duties, or I'll have to speak to you more strictly."

"I'll get even with you for this, you see if I don't!"

Hardinge was well aware that Swasey's rage stemmed from the fact that he had tried his own charm on Belle and had been thoroughly rebuffed.

"I'll get you. You can't treat me like this," Swasey muttered deep in his throat as he stalked off.

Later that night, Jeff came upon Ensign Hardinge on deck and stood aside to let him pass.

"Good evening," the ensign said. "Your name is Majors, isn't it? Jeff Majors?"

"Why, yes, it is, Ensign. I didn't think you knew it, though."

"Oh, the ship's not all that big," Hardinge said. "Have you been at sea long?"

Jeff felt a start of fear that he might be found out. "No, sir, not long."

"But you like the sea?"

"Oh, yes, sir, I like it well enough."

"Where's your home?"

"Richmond."

Hardinge continued to talk pleasantly. "My home is in Pennsylvania. Different country from around here. My folks have a big farm there."

"I come from a farm," Jeff said quickly. "Not a big one, though—just a small place."

As the two stood talking, Jeff realized that Hardinge was making no attempt to plumb his secret.

Finally the ensign asked, "Have you known Miss Leah long? Miss Belle tells me you two are old friends, so I guess you have."

"Oh, yes, we grew up very close together. Mostly in Kentucky, though."

"She's a very attractive young lady. The captain told me her brother is in the Federal army."

"Yes, sir, that's true."

Hardinge looked out over the sea, then turned back to Jeff. "I get pretty tired of this having to choose sides—the country torn right down the middle. For a young fellow like you, that's a bad way to grow up. I'll be glad when it's all over."

Despite himself, Jeff nodded. "I will too, Ensign. I guess most of us will be."

"Well, good night, Jeff."

"Good night, Ensign."

Later on Jeff spoke to Captain Bier. "You know, he's not a bad fellow—that Ensign Hardinge. We had us quite a talk on deck."

"What did you talk about?" the captain asked curiously.

"Oh, mostly just about farming. He was raised on a farm, just like I was."

"He seems to be a fine officer."

"What will happen to you, Captain?" Jeff asked then.

"Well, it may go hard with me. They know I've brought quite a few ships through the blockade. They also know I was once a member of Stonewall Jackson's staff. I'll probably wind up in a prison camp."

"That would be awful. My father was in one for a while before he got exchanged."

"Well, it's up to the Lord to get us out of things like this, so you might say a prayer for me."

Jeff hesitated. "I guess you might tell Leah that."

"You mean you don't pray, my boy?"

"I'm not very good at it." Jeff was embarrassed by the question. "Good night, Captain. I hope you don't have to go to prison."

The *Greyhound* plunged on through the Atlantic, headed north toward Boston. It was a little kingdom of its own, with Ensign Hardinge the king of the realm. His officers were the next level and then the sailors and the civilians.

And as they plowed through the sea, Belle Boyd, down in her cabin, was thinking a great deal of what she had once said: *I want a romantic courtship.*

She stretched out on her bunk and thought of Ensign Hardinge's chiseled, handsome features, his courtesy, his grace, and she sighed deeply.

"Well, this is romantic enough, even for me!"

12

Boston

The *Greyhound* covered the distance to Boston much quicker than some aboard would have chosen. Captain Bier, for example, hated the thought of arrival, for he knew that he would be transferred almost immediately to one of the prisons reserved for naval officers. It would not be a pleasant experience, and he dreaded the thought of it.

Leah and Jeff had spoken briefly about the future, but neither had any idea of what to expect. So far, no one had mentioned Jeff's being a member of the Confederate army, and they were both hopeful that this would never come out.

Lieutenant Hardinge wished that his assignment were to sail the ship all the way to the North Pole—for that would give him more time to court Belle Boyd. He was fearful for Belle's future, knowing it was entirely possible that a military court could sentence her to another term in prison.

Belle had never been charmed by a man as she had been by Sam Hardinge. She knew men very well, and—despite her apparent willfulness and oftentimes flamboyant behavior—she saw in the young sailor a man who had deep feelings and was steady and reliable. She, too, worried about her fate when they got to Boston.

They arrived at Boston harbor one morning and by noon were docked.

Belle came to Leah's cabin early, which surprised the younger girl considerably.

"I've got to talk to you, Leah," Belle said. She paced the floor nervously.

"What is it, Belle?" Leah asked. She thought for a moment and said, "Are you worried about what's going to happen to you?"

"Oh, that will be all right, I suppose," Belle said. She looked as though she had not slept well. Now she glanced up with a strange expression on her face. "What would you think," she asked slowly, "if I told you that I had fallen in love with Sam Hardinge?"

Leah's eyes opened wide, but she said almost at once, "I wouldn't be too surprised, Belle."

"You wouldn't?"

"Why, of course not. You're not such a good actress as you might think." Leah smiled. "You light up like a lamp every time he comes into the room."

"Oh, I certainly do not!"

"Yes, you do," Leah argued. "And he does the same every time he sees you."

Leah's cabin was so small that Belle had little room to pace. She picked nervously at the fabric of her dress, and a long silence ran on. "Oh, it's all foolishness, I suppose. But if he asks me to marry him, I'd have a hard time giving him an answer."

Leah was amazed. "You mean you might marry him?"

"He's a very attractive man."

"But he's not a Confederate."

"I know that, and of course that should make it impossible. But it still would be a hard matter for me to decide."

"What would your people say?"

"I know what the whole South would say," Belle said. "That I was a traitor—I'd joined myself to the enemy. And I guess they'd be right."

"Somehow I don't think of Ensign Hardinge as a bad man," Leah said gently. "As a matter of fact, he's a very good man. There are good people from the North, you know."

Belle Boyd did not answer at once.

Leah knew Belle had formed the habit of thinking of all Southerners as good and all Northerners as evil, even though she was wise enough to know that this was not so.

"Oh, Leah, I'm so unhappy!"

"Do you think that he loves you?" Leah asked cautiously.

"Yes, he does. I know he does, and that bothers me too."

"It never bothered you before. You always liked to have men in love with you. You've said so to me many times."

"And it wasn't right! Love isn't a game. I've been wrong, flirting the way I have. I know I've made some young men pretty unhappy. Now it's my turn. I suppose it's only right."

For a long time, Leah sat listening. Belle wanted to talk, and she let her feelings pour out in a way she never had before.

Finally, the Rebel Spy took out her handkerchief and dabbed at her eyes. "Look at me, crying over a man! Never thought it would come to that." She got up and left the cabin without saying another word.

"I think she really cares for him," Leah said

aloud. "But she'd be in a lot of trouble if she married him, and I guess he would be too."

Later that afternoon, Leah was walking the deck as she often did. The deck was swarming with people from Boston.

Jeff soon came up to stand beside her. "Look at that! They've all come on board to see the famous Belle Boyd."

"Oh! I thought they'd come to see the ship."

"Well, that too. The *Greyhound*'s a pretty famous ship, but it's mostly Belle they came to see, I guess. She's very famous."

Leah turned to him. "I'm worried about her. I pray they don't send her to prison."

"You'd better pray that for the captain too. He asked me to pray for him, and I told him . . ." Jeff's face fell, and he shuffled his feet slightly ". . . I told him he'd better ask you to pray for him. That you were pretty good at it."

"Why, what a nice thing to say, Jeff. It's not true, of course."

Jeff looked up. "Yes, it is true. I know it now better than I ever did."

Leah smiled and started to speak, but he interrupted. "I'm worried about the captain. He really may have to go to prison."

"I've been thinking about him too. He's such a nice man. I wish we could do something!"

"I think we ought to try," Jeff said, his face growing stubborn.

"Try what?"

"Try to get him off this ship—help him escape."

"Why, we're prisoners ourselves."

111

"Yeah, but I don't think they're gonna put us in jail." Then Jeff said cautiously, his eyes glowing, "Let's go talk to Miss Belle. She's had lots of experience, being a spy and all. I bet she can think of some way to get the captain out of here."

Leah thought for a moment, then nodded. "Well, it can't hurt to try. Let's go see her quick—before they take her away."

Belle Boyd listened to them carefully. "We've got to do something," she agreed. "Let me think about it. Ensign Hardinge told me that we'd be leaving the ship tomorrow. We'll have to do something quickly."

And here the fire and zeal that had made her famous all over the land became apparent. Her eyes glowed, and her chin looked determined. "Come along," she said. "Let's go find the captain. Something can be done, I am sure."

"I just don't think it can be done, Miss Belle." Captain Bier seemed touched that Jeff and the girls had thoughts of finding a way for him to escape, but he had little confidence that any attempt would work.

"Why, there's always a way to do things, Captain," Belle insisted. "Men get out of prison camps all the time."

"A ship is different, Miss Belle."

"No, it's just another kind of prison camp. It can be done."

"I think we ought to try, Captain," Jeff spoke up. "It'll be harder to get out of almost any prison camp than it will be to escape from the *Greyhound*."

Captain Bier scratched his chin thoughtfully. "Well, there's something in that. Those camps are

112

tough. But I still don't see how anything can be done."

Belle leaned forward and said intently, "There's a little boat on the stern of the ship."

"Yes, the dory. But getting to it would be the trouble. There will be guards on deck."

"Not too many, I think," Belle insisted.

"Nobody's really expecting you to try to escape," Leah urged. "You can catch them off guard."

"Well, let's see . . ." Captain Bier began to get interested. "There's one guard outside the door of this cabin. It's never left unguarded. You'd have to find a way to get him out of the way."

Belle smiled, her blue gray eyes gleaming. "I think I have an answer for that, Captain."

"But—how?"

"He's a man, isn't he?"

"Well, yes, but—"

"I've gotten men to do things before, Captain." Belle smiled with confidence. "That part won't be hard."

"Well, then the officers will have to be out of the way—away from the stern."

"We'll just have to hope they are." Leah nodded. "They usually stay in the bow, don't they?"

"Come to think of it, they do."

Belle thought hard, then said, "Is it hard to get the dory into the water?"

"Well, it takes a little time—and it's noisy."

"We'll have to get it down—maybe John Pollard will help."

Bier shook his head. "We'd be noticed. We couldn't do it without someone seeing us."

"Have some faith, Captain," Belle urged. "We've

113

got to try—even if we don't succeed. I can put up with anything but quitting!"

Bier's eyes gleamed with humor and admiration. "I'll bet you gave your captors a hard time when you were held in Old Capitol Prison, didn't you, Miss Belle?"

Belle laughed aloud. "I did! They were glad to be rid of me."

"What did you do, Miss Belle?" Jeff asked.

"They put me in a room on the second floor. The first day some fool of a Union officer came to force me to take the oath of allegiance. I told him to leave my quarters—and I said it loud enough so that the other prisoners heard. They cheered like anything!"

"Was it very hard—being in prison?"

"Not for me. They fed me well, and the Washington secessionists managed to smuggle all kinds of good food to me. I shared it with the others, of course. The first time Major Doster called on me, I was eating peaches and reading *Harper's* magazine. I told him that I could stay there if the Yankees could afford to keep me. It made him very angry."

"What else did you do?" Bier asked.

"Oh, I gave them a concert nearly every night— all good Southern songs, of course. I always sang 'Maryland, My Maryland,' and I sang the line 'I scorn the Northern scum' at the top of my lungs!"

"Did they try to make you stop?" Leah asked.

"Yes, but I just said, 'I shan't do it,' and sang louder."

"I don't see how you got by with it." Bier shook his head.

"I always took a broom and swept the floor

whenever the Yankee guards came in. It made them furious."

"I'll bet it did!"

"And I went to church every Sunday—but I went with a Confederate flag sewed on the bosom of my dress. Oh, my, that did insult them!"

"You're a caution, Belle Boyd," Bier said. "All right, we'll try it. Make whatever plans you can—and have John Pollard help you."

"You be ready to go at any hour." Belle got up to leave. "We'll get you out of this yet!"

"Do you really think it'll work, Belle?" Leah asked as they walked back to their cabins."

Belle smiled, her eyes gleaming. Obviously this was exactly the sort of thing she loved! "We'll do it, Leah—all we have to do is hold our heads up and show a little spunk!"

13
Captain Bier

Captain Almy of the *Connecticut* had reason to be proud of his prize. Not only would he share generously in the proceeds of the captured vessel, but the newspapers would carry the story of his capture of "The Siren of the Shenandoah," Belle Boyd.

Leaning back in his chair, Captain Almy felt very pleased with himself. He ran over again in his mind the money that would come from the seizure of the *Greyhound* and then began to write his report to Rear Admiral S. P. Lee, Commander of the North Atlantic Blockading Squadron:

> The *Greyhound* has a very valuable cargo on board of eight hundred bales of cotton, thirty-five tons of tobacco, and twenty-five casks of turpentine. She threw overboard twenty bales of cotton endeavoring to avoid capture.
>
> The captain's name is George H. Bier, whom I formerly knew as a lieutenant in the United States Navy. Now, however, he is on the Confederate Navy register as a captain.
>
> I placed officers of the prized crew on board the *Greyhound*. She is, at this moment, in Boston Harbor. Ensign Samuel Hardinge, Jr., is in charge of the ship. . . .

After he had finished writing his report, Captain Almy placed it in an envelope. He went to the sailor on guard outside his cabin door, handed him the letter, and said, "Take this and see that it gets posted."

"Aye, sir."

Boston harbor was filled with ships. He looked them over with a critical eye and then pulled a newspaper clipping from his pocket and reread it. It was dated May 20:

> The steamer had on board as passengers the famous Rebel spy Miss Belle Boyd, and Mr. Pollard of Richmond, author of a Southern history of the rebellion. Miss Boyd came on board the steamer at Wilmington as Mrs. Lewis, and her deportment on ship is described by the officers as very ladylike.

Captain Almy was a humorless man and smiled little. However, his lips turned up slightly as he considered again the fame that would come to him as the man who had captured Belle Boyd.

When Ensign Hardinge came by Almy's cabin late in the morning, he was surprised by the pleasant, almost jovial, aspect of his captain.

Leaning back in his chair, Almy stared at the ensign.

"Do you have any orders, Captain Almy?"

"No, Ensign Hardinge, not for the moment." The captain stared at the young officer for a moment longer and smiled. "How's your romance with the Rebel going?"

Ensign Hardinge flushed. He knew that the captain, as well as others on board, had been aware of his feelings for Belle Boyd. He had taken considerable teasing from the men and even from the dour Captain Almy himself.

"It's not something I'd like to joke about, sir," he said rather shortly—as shortly as he dared with his captain.

"Now, now, my boy, these things happen! She's an attractive young lady, and you're a young man. It's quite natural, I'm sure." He studied the ensign. "But impossible, of course. You know what the woman is."

"I know she's a very dedicated, beautiful young woman!" Ensign Hardinge declared.

"Dedicated? She's dedicated, all right! She's dedicated to overthrowing the government of the United States of America." His face grew stern, and he said in a voice that raked on the young officer's nerves, "Put such things out of your mind! You have a fine career ahead of you in the navy."

Hardinge bit his lip nervously. "I'm sorry you take such a dim view of it, Captain."

"I think only what everyone would think if you get involved with such a woman. I don't understand you. Don't you know what she's famous for?"

"I beg your pardon, sir?"

"Why, she eats young Union officers like a black widow spider," Almy said grimly. "She charms them, gets military information from them, and then throws them away. According to the papers, she's done it dozens of times."

"That's not the way this is, sir!"

Almy appeared shocked. "Why, Ensign, you're not serious about this woman?"

"Yes, sir, I am."

"But—but that's *impossible!*"

"No, sir, it isn't impossible."

"Why, you'd be throwing your career down the drain. Besides," he said, "chances are she'll wind up in the Old Capitol Prison again. The authorities are tired of her antics. You must surely be aware of all of this, aren't you?"

"If that did happen, sir, it wouldn't change my feelings."

Hardinge had not intended to reveal so much to the captain. He had hoped that somehow Belle would be set free and the two of them could continue their lives together. He felt sure by this time that Belle loved him, and the many obstacles to their marriage simply caused him to be all the more determined.

For a long time Almy sat arguing with his young officer. Then, obviously seeing it was an impossible situation, he threw up his hands. "Well, this is the end! I give up, Ensign! I thought you were a young man of sense and judgment, but I can see that I was mistaken. You're dismissed."

"Yes, sir."

As Hardinge walked away, he thought soberly, *Well, there goes my career in the navy. Captain Almy would never give me a good recommendation after this.*

"Belle," Leah asked, a worried look on her face, "are you still sure this will work?"

Belle Boyd's eyes gleamed with excitement. She said quickly, "I think it will, but even if it doesn't, how would we be worse off? Captain Bier won't have a chance after they take him to a prison. And you know what horrible places they are."

"That's true." Then Leah said, "The guards here aren't very alert, are they?"

"There hasn't been much need to be when we were at sea. After all, where could anyone go to out in the middle of the ocean? Now that we're on land, though, it's different."

"Can he swim?" Leah asked in a worried tone.

"I have no idea," Belle confessed. "But remember the dory. Somehow we'll have to use that. If he can just get into it, he can make his escape to shore.

"I don't know. I just don't know," Leah said. It all seemed terribly difficult to her.

"Let's go talk to Mr. Pollard," Belle said.

The two girls went at once to Pollard's cabin. He was surprised to see them, and when they stepped inside he looked at Belle carefully. "You're excited about something," he said. "I can tell by the look on your faces. What is it?"

Belle made a face. "I can't hide my feelings," she said. "Yes, I am. There's something we want to do, John."

"What is it?"

"We'd like to help Captain Bier escape."

Surprise washed over Mr. Pollard's face. "So would I, but I don't see any chance of that."

"But there is!" Belle insisted. "All we've got to do is get him off this ship. Once he gets to shore—he's a clever man. He can disguise himself, hire a wagon or a horse, and ride out of Boston. It would be a difficult trip, making his way through the lines, but he could do it."

Leah said, "Or maybe he could find a ship going away from Boston—he knows lots of sailors. Anything to get away from here! I hate to think about him going to prison—they're terrible places."

The three of them talked about Belle's plan, and finally Mr. Pollard said, "All right, we'll try it. Now let's get this all down. We'll only have one chance, Belle. Captain Almy told me they were coming to take us ashore tomorrow. So it's today—or tonight!"

The three of them sat for a long time in Mr. Pollard's cabin, planning the details of the escape.

"All right," Mr. Pollard said at last. "That's all we can do for the moment."

"But how will Captain Bier get to know all this?" Leah asked.

"I'll have to go tell him what the plan is," Pollard said. "They've been pretty good about letting me see him."

"Then tell him I said good luck," Leah said, "and that I hope to see him again."

"I'll tell him."

Pollard made his way down to the small cabin below deck where they had confined the captain. The guard admitted him without question since Captain Almy had given him permission to visit.

"Why, hello, John," Captain Bier said. "I was half expecting the guard to come and take me off to jail."

"That'll be tomorrow—if nothing happens."

Perhaps something in the way Pollard spoke aroused the captain's attention. Bier stared at him. "What's on your mind?"

"Captain, I think there's a chance for you to get away. Belle and Leah and I have worked up a scheme. If it works, you've got at least a chance."

"What about you?" Captain Bier demanded. "You need to get away too."

"Oh, they won't do anything to me. That's pretty clear, Captain. I'm not a military prisoner. But you well know how they treat the captains and officers on the blockade runners. You'd be in jail for the rest of the war."

Pollard knew the thought distressed Captain Bier. He was a man who liked the sea and the open air. The thought of being cooped up in a smelly, dank prison for perhaps years was depressing.

Bier stared at him with an eager look. "Do you have help? Are you going to seize the ship?"

"Oh, no—no! Nothing like that," Pollard protested. "Here's what we'll do . . ."

There was a great deal of excitement on the *Greyhound* and also on land. And Ensign Hardinge was giving orders here and there when one of the sailors came up to say, "Sir, we have sprung some kind of leak in the forward hull."

Hardinge turned to Belle Boyd. "I'll have to go see about this, Belle."

"Yes, John. I'll be right here."

As soon as Hardinge left, Belle turned to Leah and whispered, "It's got to be now or never!"

Leah's heart began to beat fast. Darkness was already falling. There was still a little light, just enough to see by, but it was dark enough for their purposes. They hurried to the ladder, trying to keep out of sight as much as possible. When they were below, Belle whispered, "You hide in that cabinet over there. When you hear us go by, you'll know it's time."

"All right, Belle," Leah whispered. She opened the door of what she knew to be a supply cabinet. It was so crowded with all sorts of sacks and boxes that she had to squeeze in. But she was able to see through the slats in the closed door as Belle moved down the hall. "I hope this works," she whispered. "It's got to!"

Belle approached the sailor on guard at Captain Bier's cabin door and spoke to him with a bright smile. "Good evening, sir." She thought the common sailor would be thrilled at being called "sir."

He said quickly, "Good evening, Miss Belle. Come to visit with the captain?"

"Yes, I thought I might. But tell me about yourself. Have you been in the navy long?"

The sailor appeared flattered to be interrogated by the famous Confederate spy. A short, heavyset young man, he spoke eagerly of himself.

But suddenly Belle put her hand to her head and dropped her eyes.

He cut his words off abruptly. "What's the matter, Miss Belle? Are you feeling bad?"

"Why—I do feel a little sick," she said. Then she staggered slightly. "I do think I'm going to faint—"

"I'll—you want me to get the doctor?"

"Oh, no, but . . . could you just help me back to my cabin?"

"Well . . . I'm on duty, ma'am."

"Oh, of course," Belle said. "I'll probably . . . be all right." She began to stagger away, allowing herself almost to fall.

"You—you're going to faint!"

The sailor cast a desperate look at the door—it was well secured with a heavy oak bar—then said, "Come along, Miss Belle. I can take you to your cabin. Then I'll have someone get the doctor."

"Oh, thank you. You're so kind."

Leah watched breathlessly as Belle and the sailor passed by. As soon as they had ascended the ladder, she leaped out of the closet, ran down the corridor, and lifted the oak bar. Pulling the door open, she saw Captain Bier standing there waiting.

"Come along quickly, Captain! It's dark, and Ensign Hardinge's up in the front of the ship."

"I'll make it!" The captain gave Leah a quick hug and grinned, his eyes gleaming. "Thank you, and you pass my thanks along to Miss Belle."

"I will," Leah promised, "but hurry!"

The captain ran down the corridor. He paused at the ladder, then climbed upward and peered cautiously around the deck. It was almost totally dark. Only the lights in the harbor cast their illumination over the waves. Quickly he moved to the fantail and saw that John Pollard had maneuvered the little dory off the ship. It was floating below. Quickly he stepped over the rail, jumped, and thirty seconds later was rowing desperately for shore.

Alongside the rail, John Pollard stood alone. He laughed silently when he saw the captain disappear into the darkness, then said aloud, "Well, there's one blockade runner the Yankees won't put in jail."

14
End of the Venture

The escape of Captain Bier was almost as attractive a story to the newspapers as the capture of Belle Boyd. The docks were alive with gossip. The Boston paper put it on the front page, the newsprint screaming, "CONFEDERATE BLOCKADE RUNNER ESCAPES!" The story was not at all favorable to Captain Almy, who was responsible for the security of such prisoners.

The blow had fallen heavily on the captain, and he in turn let his wrath fall on the head of Ensign Sam Hardinge.

"It's all your fault!" he shouted next morning when the young man arrived at his cabin. "I wouldn't be surprised but what you yourself turned the man loose. You won't get away with this!"

"I had nothing to do with it, sir," Ensign Hardinge protested. "I was forward—all you have to do is ask any of the crew if you doubt my word."

"Oh, don't make excuses. I know you and that Boyd woman were in it together. You made it your business," the captain snarled, "to be out of pocket, and she went down and lured that fool sailor away from the door. And I have no doubt it was Pollard —or perhaps that young girl—who let the captain out."

"I couldn't say, Captain."

"You'll regret this, Hardinge. I'm recommending that you be dismissed from the navy."

"But, sir—"

Protest as he might, Ensign Hardinge could not change the captain's mind.

Belle found Hardinge immediately after his interview with Captain Almy. She looked at his face and asked, "Is it bad, Sam?" She was surprised at how concerned she had become over his troubles.

He summoned a smile. "Well, they're not going to hang me from the yardarm—though that's pretty much what the captain would like to do, I'm sure!"

"Don't joke about it," Belle said sharply. "I know it means your career, doesn't it?"

"Yes, it does. But there are other careers." He looked at Belle and asked, "What will happen to you?"

"I think they're going to send me to Canada, just to get rid of me." She reached up and touched his cheek. "Poor Sam. You'd have been much better off if you'd never met me."

Taking her hand, he kissed it, then pulled her close. "Don't say that," he said huskily. "I love you, Belle—and all I want to know is the answer to one simple question."

"What is that?"

"Do you love me?"

Belle Boyd had found this tall young sailor possessed qualities that she had long admired in men. He was strong physically, of course, but there was also a steadfastness, a steadiness that she admired. Lacking this quality to some degree herself, she admired it when she saw it in others. She felt the honesty in him even now. She reached up, put her arms around his neck, and said, "Yes, I do love you."

"Will you marry me, Belle?"

"Yes."

He kissed her soundly, then exclaimed with joy written across his face, "Now what's a career compared with getting a wife like you?"

"They wouldn't marry us here," Belle said. "And I don't know how you'd find me in Canada."

"I'd find you no matter where they sent you," Hardinge insisted, his face bright with new happiness.

"I'll probably eventually go to England. I have business there. Could you meet me?"

"Yes, I could."

They exchanged addresses where they could get in touch. Hardinge wrote down the English address and stuck it in his waistcoat pocket. "It may take a while, but you can believe I'll be there, Belle."

Then the captain was at the door. "All right, Miss Boyd," he said stiffly, "you will go with these gentlemen. They will see that you do not make *your* escape."

"Why, Captain, I had no idea of such a thing," Belle said, smiling at Almy's angry face. "I was just saying good-bye to Ensign Hardinge." She turned to Sam again. "Good-bye, Ensign. It's been a lovely trip."

"Good-bye, Miss Belle. May the Lord go with you and bless you every step you take!"

"Why, thank you, Ensign." Belle turned to the captain, saying, "I'm ready now."

"Take her ashore," Captain Almy ordered. "If she tries to escape, you know what to do."

An army lieutenant accompanied by a heavily armed sergeant stared at the captain. "There's no need to be rude, Captain." He turned to Belle and said, "If you'll come this way, Miss Boyd, we'll see that you're well treated."

"Why, thank you, Lieutenant."

Belle stepped out on deck and walked toward the gangplank. Then she saw Leah standing at the rail and went over and embraced her.

"Good-bye, Leah. We'll meet again. I feel sure of it."

"Is everything all right, Miss Boyd?"

"Yes," Belle whispered. "I'm going to marry Sam. I wish you could be at the wedding."

"So do I," Leah whispered. "He's such a good man."

Then Belle Boyd moved on, speaking to Jeff and Mr. Pollard on her way to the gangplank.

Leah, Jeff, and Mr. Pollard watched as Belle descended the gangplank with an air of confidence and got into a carriage accompanied by the lieutenant and the sergeant.

"Well," Jeff said, "she's some woman."

"She is that!" Mr. Pollard agreed. "But I don't think she'll be doing much more spying for the Confederacy."

"Why not?" Leah asked.

"Too famous." Mr. Pollard shook his head. "Everybody knows her now. There've been pictures in all the papers. Every Union officer in the army knows about Belle Boyd. It would be impossible for her to charm information out of any of the rest of them."

"I don't know about that," Jeff said with a grin. "Seems like they all fall for Belle."

"And what will happen to you, Mr. Pollard?" Leah said suddenly.

"Oh, they're going to turn me loose. All they have against me is that I wrote a book about the Confederacy. But that's no crime. They may not like it, but they can't hang me for it!"

"I'm glad for that!" Leah said.

"What about you two?"

"We've got to get back. I need to get back to Richmond," Jeff said.

"I'm going to go to Kentucky," Leah said abruptly.

Jeff stared at her and exclaimed, "Kentucky! You're going back home?"

"Yes, I need to see my parents. Dad hasn't been well, as you know, for a long time." She hesitated, then an idea formed in her mind, and she said, "Jeff, why don't you go with me?"

"Why, I couldn't do that!"

"Why not?" Leah asked. "You haven't seen your baby sister in a long time."

Jeff thought about it. "That's right, but—"

"And if you got to Kentucky, Jeff, it'd be easy to get back to Richmond from there."

"That's not a bad idea, Leah," Mr. Pollard said. "Since Kentucky is a border state, it would be easy to travel." He reached into his pocket, pulled out his wallet, and extracted some bills. "Here! You'd better take this for your journey. You may need it. I don't suppose either of you has any money."

"Why, we couldn't take this, Mr. Pollard," Leah exclaimed.

"Take it! Take it!" Mr. Pollard insisted. "You'll need it to get to Kentucky."

Neither Leah nor Jeff protested much more. They did need money, and going back to Kentucky did seem to be the thing for Leah to do.

Leah talked with Jeff about Kentucky until they were ready to leave the *Greyhound*, finally saying simply, "Jeff, please come with me."

"Well, I still don't know." He rubbed his chin thoughtfully. "I really need to get straight back to the army. I may even be posted as a deserter."

"Mr. Pollard will take care of all that," Leah said. "You know how much influence he has. Please, Jeff." When she saw he was wavering, she said, "I'd really feel safer if you came with me."

"Safer?"

"Yes, you know it's not safe for a young woman to travel alone."

Actually she was not afraid but knew this would appeal to him.

Jeff blinked. "Why, I never thought of that!" he said.

Apparently it did not occur to him that Leah had made the trip alone from Richmond to Wilmington and that she had made other trips by herself.

She watched as he thought about it and finally drew a sigh of relief when he said, "Well, all right, we'll go to Kentucky then. I'd sure like to see Esther and your folks too."

Leah wanted to jump up and down with excitement. "Oh, Jeff! That'll be so good, and you'll get to see your home again. Won't that be wonderful?"

Jeff's face clouded. "I don't know if I've got a home anymore—just the Confederate army, I guess. I think all the time about that place where I grew up, but we'll never live there again."

"Never say never," Leah said firmly.

As they talked excitedly about the trip, Leah said, "And it'll be good to see Ezra again, won't it?"

Ezra Payne was a Yankee soldier who had escaped from Belle Isle Prison. Leah had saved his life by hiding him. She and Jeff had then helped him flee to Kentucky. According to all reports, he had taken over the Carter farm during her father's absences and was doing a fine job.

"I guess so," Jeff said shortly, giving Leah an odd look. Some of the happiness seemed to have drained from him. "Well," he said, "I guess we can leave the ship anytime."

Leah had not missed Jeff's reaction to her mention of Ezra.

She resolved to say no more about that young man. "I'll get together what few things I have— which isn't much. Maybe there's a train we can take. I like train rides, don't you?"

Jeff and Leah left Boston late that afternoon. As their train made its clickity-clack noise over the rails headed south, they sat together talking of all that had happened.

"Leah, do you think Ensign Hardinge will marry Belle?"

"Oh, yes," Leah answered at once. "Belle told me she loves him and he loves her."

"I don't see how they're going to make it," Jeff said. "Too many things against it."

131

"Why not?"

"Why, they're so different. She's Confederate, and he's Union."

"But he's a man, and she's a woman, and the war won't last forever."

But Jeff was moody. He stared out the window into the darkness for a while and then shook his head. "Think what the people from the South will say—that she's a traitor."

Leah stared at him. "I guess they'll say the same thing about Ensign Hardinge in the North."

"Sure they will. You know how people feel about things like that."

Now it was Leah who seemed depressed. "I'd like for it to be a happy ending, like in books."

"You mean," Jeff said slowly, "like 'they got married and lived happily ever after'?"

"Well, something like that."

"I don't think it happens like that too often," Jeff said.

He admired the sweep of her jaw and thought again of how much she had grown up in the past year. He wanted to say more, but somehow he felt constrained. As they headed through the darkness, he wondered what would happen to the two of them.

Leah had her long thoughts too. She still felt estranged from Jeff. There was not the closeness between them that there once had been, and she was hurt by it.

When we get home, she thought, *back to Kentucky, it'll be different. Jeff will be his old self again.*

15
Kentucky Home

The train ride turned out to be unpleasant. Hour after hour the steam locomotive chuffed along, sending black smoke high into the air. The weather was hot, and the windows were all open. This meant that cinders and soot from the wood-burning engine were sometimes swept inside, blackening the faces of the passengers.

"Ow!" Leah protested. She reached up and grabbed her face. "That hurt!"

Jeff felt tired, but it was difficult to sleep on the noisy train. He studied Leah for a moment, then said, "You've got soot all over your face."

"So've you." She dabbed at her face with a handkerchief that was already smeared, then looked at it with disgust. "I'll sure be glad to get off this old train," she complained. "I don't think we're ever going to get there!"

"It beats walking," Jeff said grimly, "or even riding a wagon. It'd take us a long time to get to Kentucky that way."

"Well, it may be faster," Leah said, "but I don't have to like it! I'd rather ride in a wagon!"

The train was packed. A woman with two small children sat across from them, and the children, no more than three and four, were tired and cried often.

Leah took the little girl on her lap from time to time and played simple games with her and told her stories.

Jeff, taking the hint, took the boy on his own lap so that the mother could stretch her legs and get a little relief.

"You're very good with children," the woman said, smiling at both of them. Her face was lined with fatigue. The journey had worn her down. "You must have brothers and sisters of your own."

Jeff looked up. "I've got a little sister even younger than these two," he said. "We're on our way to Kentucky."

"Are you brother and sister?" the woman asked.

"Oh, no," Leah said quickly. She bounced the little girl upon her knee, which caused the child to utter happy cries. "We grew up together is all. Our families own neighboring farms."

"Nice to have good friends, isn't it?" the woman said.

Jeff thought she seemed to be rather lonely.

"Are you from the North?" Leah asked. The woman's accent was somewhat different from that of Southern people.

"Yes, I'm from Massachusetts. I'm going down to visit my husband. He was wounded, and I'm coming to bring him home again. He's been paroled."

"Well, that's good," Jeff said. "He won't have to fight anymore then."

That was the custom on both sides. When a man gave his "parole," in effect he promised never to serve again in the army.

The woman's face grew a little sad, and she nodded. "He won't have to fight, but he couldn't anyway. You see, he lost a leg."

"Oh, I'm so sorry," Leah said, "but at least you'll have him back, and he's all right otherwise."

"Yes. He'll have to learn a new trade, though. He was a surveyor, and now he can't walk."

Leah and Jeff exchanged glances. The war had wrecked so many lives and so many families.

Later, when the woman had gotten off the train, Leah murmured, "I feel sorry for them."

"So do I, but at least he's alive. You can always get an artificial leg, but when you're dead, you're dead!"

At one point the train filled up with soldiers being transported somewhere—all Union, of course. They filled the car with smoke, some of them smoking pipes, others cigars. They were loud and boisterous.

After a while, Jeff said, "You know, Leah, these fellows talk kind of funny, but they're really just like the men in my brigade."

"Are they, Jeff?"

He nodded. "Sure. And look how young most of 'em are. Just like us."

"I guess there's really no difference between those that wear blue and those that wear gray."

"I never thought of that much before," Jeff said, his face thoughtful. "It's hard to feel that way when they're shooting at you and you're shooting back. But these fellows—why, they could have come from our hometown, couldn't they, Leah?"

"Yes, they could."

The journey continued for two days with the train stopping, it seemed, every five miles. Finally, however, the engine chuffed into a small station, and the conductor came through saying, "Pineville! All off for Pineville!"

"Here we are, Jeff!" Leah's eyes shone with excitement.

She grabbed her suitcase, and he picked up the knapsack he had put his few possessions in. They stepped off and stood on the platform until the train pulled away. Only two other people got off, and the station was vacant.

Leah said, "Look! There's Charlie Taylor. Maybe he'd know somebody that's going out to the farm."

They went over to the station agent, a tall, gray-haired man, who was surprised to see them. He put down the sack he was carrying and gave them a smile. "Why, Leah! And if it ain't Jeff Majors! What in the world you doing here?"

They did not tell the agent a great deal but did discover that a neighbor—a man named Bates—was in town, one who lived close to Leah's family.

"Thanks, Mr. Taylor," Jeff said. "We'll go see if we can find him. We need a ride home."

They found the neighbor, and after telling a part of their story, Leah asked, "Are you going back home again soon, Mr. Bates?"

"Sure am!" Bates exclaimed. He was a short, chunky man with red hair. "And, yes, you can ride along. My, won't your folks be surprised to see you! They don't know you're coming?"

"No, we didn't know ourselves when we'd get here."

"Well, ain't that fine now! Here, Jeff, you help me get these groceries in the back of the wagon, and we'll be on our way."

"Sure, Mr. Bates."

Ten minutes later they were moving along the road, the wagon wheels sending a column of dust rising in the air behind them. It was a beautiful day in May, and both Jeff and Leah were anxious to get to the farm, but it was a slow process.

Every time Mr. Bates met someone, he would stop for a moment, saying, "Look here! It's Leah Carter and Jeff Majors come home. Ain't that fine!"

After this had happened a half dozen times, Jeff said, "Mr. Bates, why don't you just drive on to the farm, and we'll have time to meet all these folks tomorrow?"

Bates blinked with surprise. "Why, sure. I guess you *are* anxious to see your folks. Sorry 'bout that." He slapped the lines on the backs of the horses, saying, "Giddup, Tony! Giddup, Babe!" and the team broke into a fast trot.

The Carter farm was five miles outside of town. As they pulled within sight of it, Leah exclaimed, "Look! There's Ma out in the yard, hanging up clothes!"

"She'll be surprised to see you." Mr. Bates grinned. He drove the team into the yard at a fast gallop, raising a cloud of dust. When he pulled up, he called out, "Look what I brought you! Special delivery, Miz Carter!"

Mrs. Carter had blonde hair and green eyes just like her daughter's. She was wearing a simple brown dress, and her hair was done up in braids around her head. She took one look at the young people falling out of the wagon and cried, "Leah! Jeff! My stars above!" She ran and embraced them both and then called out, "Sarah, look who's here!"

Then she turned back, saying, "What in the world are you two doing here?"

"It's a long story, Ma," Leah said, obviously very happy to be home. "I'll tell you all about it—" She stopped as Sarah came out of the house, and she ran to greet her.

Sarah Carter, at eighteen, was one of the prettiest girls in the mountains. She had dark hair, dark blue eyes, and a lovely complexion. She threw her arms around Leah and then gave Jeff a hug. "What are you two doing, dropping out of the skies?" she exclaimed.

"We came to get something to eat." Jeff grinned broadly.

Mrs. Carter laughed. "I never saw you when you weren't hungry. Come on in! That baby sister of yours has grown like a weed."

They found Leah's sister Morena sitting on the floor playing with Esther, Jeff's sister. Morena was blonde and green-eyed like Leah, but she had never developed mentally. Though she was nine years old now, she had never spoken, and the Carters accepted her as she was.

Leah ran and hugged her. "Why, Morena, look how pretty you are," she said. She stroked the girl's hair, looked down into the vacant eyes, and held her tight.

Jeff fell on his knees beside Esther, who was seated on the floor, staring up with dark brown eyes. Then he snatched her up and tossed her to the ceiling. "Look at you, Esther!" Soon he had her laughing and screaming with joy as she always did when he threw her in the air.

Then Jeff held her tightly and said, "I wish Pa and Tom could see you! They'd think you're something!"

Mrs. Carter stood back, watching Jeff hold the baby. "Yes, it's sad for a family to be apart like this," she said. "But come now. It's too early for dinner, but we've got some biscuits, and I can fix some eggs."

"Sounds good to me," Jeff said. "You got any of that good sausage—the hot kind you always make, Mrs. Carter? You know I'm real partial to that!"

"I think I can find some! You sit down now and tell us what all's been going on."

They had just sat down at the table when steps sounded on the porch.

The door opened, and a tall young man wearing a straw hat and overalls came in. Then he stopped abruptly. "Why, Leah!" he exclaimed, and his face broke into a smile.

Leah jumped up and ran to him. She took his hands. "I bet you didn't expect to have company for dinner, did you, Ezra?" she teased.

"Sure didn't. Where'd you spring from?" Ezra turned to Jeff, and his face lit up again. He walked over and stuck his hand out. "Jeff! By jingo, it's good to see you again."

"Good to see you, Ezra," Jeff mumbled. "How you been?"

"Real good. Real good. Learning how to be a farmer."

"Don't let him tell you that," Sarah said quickly. "He's already a better farmer than most men that've been at it for forty years around here."

"That's right," Mrs. Carter said. She gave the young man an affectionate look and added, "Sit down, Ezra. You might as well eat too."

Ezra took his seat, his eyes fastened on Leah. "You sure look good," he said simply.

"Oh, I'm all over soot from that old train. I can't wait to take a bath," she protested.

"Well, you look good to me," he said. "You too, Jeff."

Jeff had mixed feelings about Ezra Payne. He had learned to like the young man as they helped him make his escape from Virginia. But the truth was, he was somewhat jealous because of Leah's feelings for him.

Ezra ate hungrily as Leah told the story of the blockade-running expedition and the capture of Belle Boyd.

"You really met Belle Boyd?" Sarah said. "What was she like?"

"Oh, you'd like her, Sarah," Leah said quickly. "She's real nice."

"And you say she's going to marry that Yankee officer?"

"Yes, isn't that romantic?"

Jeff stared at Leah and shook his head. He was still doubtful about the whole business of Belle's marriage to young Hardinge. "I think it's a mistake," he said. He talked around a huge mouthful of eggs. "I think they're both crazy. It'll never work."

"Why you say that, Jeff?" Ezra said. "If they love each other, it'll be all right."

"No, it won't," Jeff argued. "He's a Yankee, and she's a Confederate. How you gonna put those two things together?"

Then he saw the pain that came into Sarah's face. *She's so in love with Tom—and she sees that she probably will never get him. I wonder what she thinks about Belle marrying a Yankee.*

It was Ezra who brought the matter up. He looked at Sarah and said, "Well, I guess if Belle Boyd can marry a Yankee, Tom can marry you, can't he, Miss Sarah?"

Sarah grew pale. She probably wished that the subject had not come up, for she had struggled with this problem ever since Jeff's brother joined the Confederate army.

"I don't think it would work for me. Belle's different."

"I don't see how she's any different," Ezra said, puzzled. "Seems to me, when people love each other —why, that's a whole lot more important than politics."

"You just don't know what you're talking about, Ezra," Jeff said sharply.

Ezra flinched at Jeff's sudden attack. "Well, I probably don't," he said and looked down and began eating slowly.

"Oh, let's have a good time," Leah said quickly. "We don't have to talk about the war, do we?"

"That's a good idea, Leah. Let's talk about going to church tomorrow. My, won't Brother Jenkins be surprised to see you! And all the neighbors will be stopping by!"

"Oh, I've missed my church," Leah said.

"Didn't you have a good church there in Richmond?"

"Oh, yes," Leah said, "but not like here." She had grown up in the little white frame church building, had become a believer there, and almost every day thought about that part of her life.

"Well, it's mostly women there now, with the men gone off to war," her mother said.

They talked about the church, and Jeff ate silently, feeling somewhat out of place.

Later that afternoon, Jeff was just walking around the farm aimlessly when Leah caught up with him.

"Let's go down to the creek, Jeff. We can catch some fish for supper."

Jeff looked at her. He wanted to go, but there was a stubbornness in him. Somehow he still resented Ezra Payne, although he would have died rather than say so.

"Why don't you and Ezra go?" he said.

"Ezra? Why, Ezra can fish anytime. Besides, I want to go with you."

Jeff brightened. "All right," he said, and they ran to the barn to get the poles. Then they dug a canful of worms and soon were sitting on the riverbank. The fish were biting, and before long they had a string of nice punkin-seed perch.

"Maybe later we can go down to the bridge and see if Old Napoleon's still there."

Old Napoleon was the tremendous bass that Jeff had spent a great deal of time trying to catch. He had actually landed him once.

"You remember when you caught Old Napoleon the last time we went there?"

"Sure, I remember."

Leah turned to him. "You turned him loose, Jeff. Why'd you do that?"

Jeff found it hard to put into words what he was thinking. "Well, someday I'd like to come back here, and I'd like for things to be like they were. I guess I thought if I could just leave Napoleon there, that'd make it like old times."

"That's nice, Jeff," Leah whispered. She was sitting very close, and she leaned over and touched his shoulder. "We can do all the things we used to do: go fishing, hunt birds' eggs, go coon hunting . . ."

The sun was setting in the west, throwing red gleams over the water in the creek. A school of minnows flashed down at their feet, silver arrows that darted and stirred up the sand in the creek bottom.

Jeff sat silently for a while, then shook his head. "I don't know if we can ever go back to being what we were."

"What do you mean?"

"Well, things change, Leah. We were just kids then. We can't go back to being ten years old again."

"Why, no . . . I wouldn't want that!"

Jeff waited till his cork disappeared with a plop, then quickly jerked a wiggling perch out of the water. He removed the hook carefully and put the fish on the stringer. Only then did he turn to her and say, "I don't know. Those were good days—no war, nobody gettin' killed. All we did was have fun, seems like. Can't go back and do that again."

"Don't be sad, Jeff." Leah put her hand on his. "We can't be ten years old again, but it's pretty nice being fifteen."

He looked down at her hand. It was strong and tan. Then he looked over at her, saying quietly, "Maybe you're right. I sure hope so."

The two went back to the house, Jeff carrying the stringer of fish. They said no more about the way things used to be, but Leah knew that Jeff was not happy. Once again she felt that wall between them building and didn't know why. As they walked along, she wanted to break through it, but his face was set, and she didn't know what to say.

16
Last Ride

Jeff sat on the straight-backed pew, listening intently to Brother Jenkins. Church brought back so many memories! Looking over the congregation, he saw familiar faces going all the way back to his childhood. Sitting beside him was Leah, and on her right was Ezra Payne. The rest of the family was on his left.

Leah's father sat next to Jeff. He was a thin man with brown hair and faded blue eyes. His mouth was firm under a scraggly mustache, and he smiled now at Jeff.

He doesn't look good, Jeff thought. *I know Leah's worried about him—and Mrs. Carter too.*

Mr. Carter held his Bible on his knees, following the reading of the Scripture by Brother Jenkins. His Bible was worn almost to pieces through constant reading.

The minister finished his Scripture reading and looked over the congregation. "We're happy today," he said pleasantly, "to have Jeff Majors and Leah Carter back home. Always good to see our folks coming back." Then he said, "Now, for the message this morning, I've chosen the subject 'Judge not, that ye be not judged.'"

The next hour turned out to be one of the most difficult hours of Jeff Majors's life. He had known heartache when his family had decided to move to Virginia. That had been hard indeed—leaving all the things he'd grown up with, the people, the places, the good times. It had been difficult when his father had been captured and sent to a Federal prison, and it had been difficult leaving Esther with another family.

But somehow, as Brother Jenkins preached on "Judge not . . ." Jeff felt himself turning completely miserable. He was a Christian, had trusted Jesus without doubt, and served God as best he could. But the words of Scripture "Judge not, that ye be not judged" seemed like an arrow in his heart.

Jeff could not help but think how bitterly he had lashed out at Leah. He tried to ignore the bitterness that had been in him—and still was in him, he knew—but before his mind came the memory of how he had flared out in anger over that scene between Leah and Cecil Taylor.

Judge not, that ye be not judged.

It seemed that Brother Jenkins was looking right down into his heart. Jeff squirmed and could not meet the minister's eyes. He stared at his hands and saw that they were tightly clenched. *What's the matter with me?* he thought.

But really, he knew. There had been uneasiness and unhappiness in him ever since he had blown up at Leah. Now, as the words of the Scripture hit him like a hammer, he suddenly realized, *Why, that's what's the matter with me! I've been judging Leah, and I'm no better than she is. Not as good, I reckon.*

His hands clenched and unclenched, and he feared Leah could feel him twisting on the bench beside her.

The sermon ended after what seemed an interminable time. As Jeff passed out of the church,

Brother Jenkins put his hand out and shook Jeff's. He was smiling. "So good to have you back, my boy. I've missed you—we all have."

"Thank you, Brother Jenkins. That was a . . . a good sermon."

Pastor Jenkins seemed to notice the hesitation in Jeff's voice. He was a very wise man and had learned how to read small signs. "The Scripture's very clear on that subject, isn't it?" He paused, then added, "So many times I've caught myself judging people. Then I realized that I'm no man to judge anyone—that God's our judge. But," he said, smiling and pressing Jeff's hand hard, "all we have to do is go to God. He forgives us for that as well as for every other sin."

"I reckon that's so, isn't it?"

"'Course it is!" Jenkins slapped Jeff across the shoulder. "Now, you enjoy your visit here!"

The Carter family went home, and Jeff said almost nothing on the way. Then he played with Esther, sitting on the floor of the parlor, listening as the family talked but taking no part in the conversation.

At dinner that day—which was cold chicken and vegetables—Dan Carter thanked God for the safety of the children. He prayed for Tom and for Jeff's father and for his own son serving in the Union army. Finally he said, "God, we're in Your hands. May we never step aside from what You've commanded us to do. Most of all, may we love one another with all of our hearts."

After dinner, Jeff went outside. He walked until he came to an old tree he had climbed many times as a young boy. Looking up at the big branches, he stood thinking of the sermon. And then he said, "God, I'm sorry I've been so hateful to Leah. I ask You to forgive me for it. That's all I know to do." He hesitated, then added, "I'll try to do better, I promise." He prayed for a while, then put on his hat on and walked back to the house, determined that things would be different.

The next morning, Jeff said, "Come along, Leah. We're going for a ride."

"For a ride?"

"Sure." He grinned. "We're going out to find that woodpecker egg that you never did add to your collection."

Leah flashed a smile at him. "Let me put on some old overalls," she said. "I can't ride like this."

Jeff went to the barn and led out one of the horses, an older horse named Feathers. He was brown, but there were white markings on his flank that looked like feathers. He didn't put a saddle on Feathers, and when Leah came out he said, "Bareback today, Leah!"

"That's fine. Just like old times."

Jeff put his hands down and said, "Here, step up!"

Leah put her foot in his hands, and he easily lifted her. She swung her leg over, sat down, and then took the reins.

Jeff leaped up behind her with an easy motion, and she said, "I don't see how you do that!"

"I've been doing it a long time. I guess you can do the steering. I'll just hang on back here."

Leah turned the horse out of the lot, and they went galloping down the road.

"What's your hurry?" Jeff called. He put his

hands on her waist to steady himself. "You're gonna shake me off back here!"

Leah shook her hair back. She had not tied it up, and it flew in Jeff's face. It smelled good, and he knew she had just washed it with rainwater. "Your hair's getting in my face," he protested, although it was not an unpleasant sensation.

Leah merely laughed and kicked her heels against Feathers's sides. "We've got a long way to go."

It was a fine day. The sun was shining, and they rode over the old familiar places, crossing creeks, going down hidden trails, laughing, and finally—to their surprise—they did find the precious woodpecker egg.

Jeff had climbed up in a dead pine tree that had a few limbs left. Peering inside a small hole, he breathed, "Leah, I think we've got it at last!"

"I want to see. Wait for me, Jeff!" Leah tied Feathers firmly, then came to the tree. She made the first limb easily enough but could not climb to the second.

"Here, take my hand," Jeff said. Leaning over, he held onto a limb with his right hand, took both of hers, and heaved her up. Then both were standing on the same limb, rather precariously.

"Look down in there. That's it!" he said.

"Oh, Jeff! We've looked for that for years!"

"I don't think I can get my hand in there. Can you?"

Leah reached out carefully. The hole was very small. "I can do it!" she said.

She forced her hand through the hole, groped down, and touched a tiny egg. "I hope I don't break it getting it out," she said.

Jeff was holding her so that she wouldn't fall. He was again very much aware of the scent of her freshly washed hair.

Slowly she pulled her hand out, then opened it. "There it is!" she said. She looked up at him. "Now! Are you happy?"

Jeff ducked his head, "Well, I'm glad about the egg. We hunted for it a long time. I think about those times a lot."

A soft wind was blowing through the trees, making a whispering noise. It blew Leah's hair, and she shook her head to make it fall down over her shoulders. "I think about those days too, Jeff." She held the woodpecker egg carefully in her palm, studying it. "We must have climbed a hundred trees, looking for an egg like this. Now we have it!"

"Better get down before we fall," he said. But then he hesitated. "Before we get down, I want to tell you something."

"Yes?"

"Well, I'm sorry that I've been such a pest." It was hard for him to apologize, especially with her large blue-green eyes fixed on him. He swallowed hard. "I was wrong to get mad at you about Cecil. Sorry, Leah."

Leah's face lit up. "Oh, Jeff, I want us to be just like we used to be."

"Well, I was wrong. Can you forgive me?"

"Of course, I can."

"I guess," he said slowly, "I was just . . . well . . . jealous, you might say."

Leah smiled suddenly. "Jealous?"

"Well, yes. Cecil comes from a fine family, and they've got money. He knows how to dress. All I know how to do is beat on an old drum."

"That's not so," Leah said. She was holding the egg in one hand, and he was still steadying her. Reaching up, she touched his hair and pushed a lock of it back off his forehead in an affectionate gesture. "I don't want to hear you talk about yourself like that." She smiled. "Now we've got that all out of the way—and we've got a woodpecker egg!"

Jeff looked down into her eyes and smiled too. His voice was filled with relief as he said, "Well, I'm glad that's over. Now we can be friends just the way we used to be." A mischievous light came into his eyes, and he said, "Leah?"

"Yes, Jeff?"

"Don't you think at a time like this there should be some sort of . . . physical gesture? I mean, after all, that's the way it's done in all the books."

"Physical gesture?" Leah asked, puzzled. "What do you mean?"

"I mean . . . like . . ." Jeff hesitated, then swallowed hard. "I mean, like maybe a kiss?"

Leah flushed and said sharply, "Why, Jeff! I'm surprised at you."

"Well, I mean, it's just the way they do in the books."

"What books have you been reading?" she teased. Reaching up, she pulled his head down and kissed him on the cheek and said, "There!"

"Well," Jeff said slowly, "I guess that's better than nothing. After all, you don't have much experience kissing."

"And you do?" she said almost angrily.

Jeff laughed aloud. "No, I don't. But anyhow, thanks for the kiss. Now let's get down from here before this limb breaks."

As soon as they were on the ground, Leah looked around and said, "You know, this is a nice place, isn't it?"

"Sure is."

"Come on, let's go back home."

As they mounted Feathers, she turned around to say, "Will you be going back to the army soon?"

"Sure, I'll have to get back. But you know—" he spoke slowly "—somehow I don't feel so bad this time. Now that we're all right again, things don't seem so bad. It's good to have a best friend."

"And you're not jealous anymore?"

"Well, I guess I am a little—maybe of Ezra. You like him a lot?"

"Why, of course." She smiled and squeezed his arm. "But he's not like you. Best friends, Jeff?"

Jeff Majors put his hand over hers and squeezed it. It was a long way back to Richmond. There was still a war to fight. Tomorrow was uncertain. But looking down into Leah's blue-green eyes, he was able to say, "Best friends always, Leah."

The Bonnets and Bugles Series includes: